MY CHILDREN'S CHILDREN

MY CHILDREN'S CHILDREN

by
LESLIE RICE

XULON PRESS

Xulon Press
2301 Lucien Way #415
Maitland, FL 32751
407.339.4217
www.xulonpress.com

Unless otherwise indicated, Scripture quotations taken from the New American Standard Bible (NASB). Copyright © 1960, 1962, 1963, 1968, 1971, 1972, 1973, 1975, 1977, 1995 by The Lockman Foundation. Used by permission. All rights reserved.

Paperback ISBN-13: 978-1-6628-3387-8
Hard Cover ISBN-13: 978-1-6628-3388-5
eBook ISBN-13: 978-1-6628-3389-2

DEDICATION

This book is dedicated to my family: first, to my husband, Steve. Over fifty-two years ago as teenagers, we chose each other to travel the path of life together. God intervened in our lives and changed us, and our path forever. It has been intense in so many ways, and so rewarding. Thank you, Steve, for all the sacrifices you have made for me and our children. Thank you for your support and encouragement to walk with God. Each of our children are a unique gift from God: Gwendolyn, who I look forward to getting to know in heaven; Adam, our intense and truth seeking first son; Carrie, our gentle and kind light; and David, a faithful and loyal heart who seeks to live a life of integrity. Each of you is precious to us for who God made you to be. You all have contributed to me as a human being in inestimable ways and have loved and supported me, for which I will always be grateful. You have brought your loves, Tonya and Bruce, into our little tribe and multiplied the blessings with your children. It is for you and them that I write this book. We are living in momentous times. You were born for such a time as this. Be ready.

Holy Father, I praise you and adore you. This is my sacrifice to you; my attempt to follow the leading of Your Spirit and to be faithful to the end. May You be glorified in it. I pray You will anoint it and make it useful for Your kingdom.

TABLE OF CONTENTS

8 "The Lord planted a garden toward the east, in Eden; and there He placed the man He had formed. 9 Out of the ground the Lord caused to grow every tree that is pleasing to the sight and good for food; the tree of life also in the midst of the garden, and the tree of the knowledge of good and evil... 16 The Lord God commanded the man, saying, 'From any tree of the garden you may eat freely; 17 but from the tree of the knowledge of good and evil you shall not eat, for in the day that you eat from it you will surely die. 18 Then the Lord God said, 'It is not good for man to be alone; I will make him a helper suitable for him.'"

3:1 "Now the serpent was more crafty than any beast of the field which the Lord God had made. And he said to the woman, 'Indeed, has God said, 'You shall not eat from any tree of the garden?' 2 The woman said to the serpent, 'From the fruit of the trees of the garden we may eat; 3 but from the fruit of the tree which is in the middle of the garden, God has said, 'You shall not eat from it or touch it, or you will die.' 4 The serpent said to the woman, 'You surely will not die! 5 For God knows that in the day you eat from it your eyes will be opened, and you will be like God, knowing good and evil.' 6 When the woman saw that the tree was good for food, and that the tree was desirable to make one wise, she took from its fruit and ate; and she gave also to her husband with her, and he ate... 8 And they heard the sound of the Lord God walking in the garden in the cool of the day, and the man and his wife hid themselves from the presence of the Lord God among the trees of the garden."

Job 1:6-12

> "Now there was a day when the sons of God came to present themselves before the LORD, and Satan also came among them. The LORD said to Satan, "From where do you come?" Then Satan answered the LORD and said, 'From roaming about on the earth and walking around on it.'
>
> The LORD said to Satan, 'Have you considered My servant Job? For there is no one like him on the earth, a blameless and upright man, fearing God and turning away from evil.'
>
> Then Satan answered the LORD, 'Does Job fear God for nothing? Have you not made a hedge about him and his house and all that he has, on every side? You have blessed the work of his hands, and his possessions have increased in the land. But put forth Your hand now and touch all that he has; he will surely curse you to your face.'
>
> Then the LORD said to Satan, 'Behold, all that he has is in your power, only do not put forth your hand on him.' So Satan departed from the presence of the LORD." ...

Job 1:20-22

> "Then Job arose and tore his robe and shaved his head, and he fell to the ground and worshiped. He said, 'Naked I came from my mother's womb, and naked I shall return there. The LORD gave and the LORD has taken away. Blessed be the name of the LORD.' Through all this Job did not sin nor did he blame God."

Job 2:1-7

"Again there was a day when the sons of God came to present themselves before the LORD, and Satan also came among them to present himself before the LORD. The LORD said to Satan, 'Where have you come from?' Then Satan answered the LORD and said, 'From roaming about on the earth and walking around on it.' The LORD said to Satan, 'Have you considered My servant Job? For there is no one like him on the earth, a blameless and upright man fearing God and turning away from evil. And he still holds fast to his integrity, although you incited Me against him to ruin him without cause.'

Satan answered the LORD and said, 'Skin for skin! Yes, all that a man has he will give for his life. However, put forth Your hand now and touch his bone and his flesh; he will curse you to your face.' So the LORD said to Satan, 'Behold, he is in your power, only spare his life.'

Then Satan went out from the presence of the LORD and smote Job with sores and boils from the soles of his foot to the crown of his head."...

Job 42:10, 12

"The Lord restored the fortunes of Job when he prayed for his friends, and the Lord increased all that Job had twofold...The LORD blessed the latter days of Job more than his beginning;..."

Hebrews 1:13-14

"But to which of the angels has He ever said, 'SIT AT MY RIGHT HAND, UNTIL I MAKE YOUR ENEMIES A

FOOTSTOOL FOR YOUR FEET?' Are they [angels] not all ministering spirits, sent to render service for the sake of those who will inherit salvation [man]?' "

<u>Hebrews 2: 5-8</u>

"For He did not subject to angels the world to come, concerning which we are speaking. But one has testified somewhere, saying, 'What is man, that you remember him? Or the son of man, that you are concerned about him? You have made him for a little while lower than the angels; You have crowned him with glory and honor, and have appointed him over the works of Your hands; You have put all things in subjection under his feet.' For in subjecting all things to him, He left nothing that is not subject to him. But now we do not yet see all things subjected to him." 2:9 But we do see Him who was made for a little while lower than the angels, namely, Jesus, because of the suffering of death crowned with glory and honor, so that by the grace of God He might taste death for everyone. 10 For it was fitting for Him, for whom are all things, and through whom are all things, in bringing many sons to glory, to perfect the author of their salvation through sufferings..." 14 "Therefore, since the children share in flesh and blood, He Himself likewise also partook of the same, that through death He might render powerless him who had the power of death, that is, the devil, 15 and might free those who through fear of death were subject to slavery all their lives. 16 For assuredly He does not give help to angels, but He gives help to the descendant of Abraham. 17 Therefore He had to be made like His brethren in all things, so that He might become a merciful and faithful high priest in things pertaining to God, to make propitiation for the sins of the people. 18 For since He Himself was tempted in that which He has suffered, He is able to come to the aid of those who are tempted."

———— ⟫⟪⟨●⟩⟫ ————

BEGINNINGS

"I guess it was a lot harder than I ever thought it would be."

"You'd thought about it beforehand?"

"Sure. After we talked about it, and you asked if I would go."

"Do you regret it?"

"No, it's just not easy. I didn't imagine how hard it would be in their reality."

"Hard for whom? You or them?"

"Both of us, I guess. They hid from me, you know. They were afraid of me. It was so strange after the time we had spent hanging, and just talking. They just loved being there and loved each other, and loved the homestead and critters. I had to smile at some of the names they came up with. But afterward, when they listened to the lies of Lucifer, they tried to avoid responsibility for it, even tried to throw each other under the bus, saying it wasn't their fault. Boy, things took a turn real fast."

"Did you take care of it?"

"Well, kind of. He released them to me, but wanted some payment right then. So I butchered some of the critters for a down payment. He didn't seem satisfied. Said he'd let them go for now, but made a claim on their kids—all of them. Every last one of them. I wanted to end it right then. I had to restrain myself, but I did make him eat dirt, the scum."

"Greed and pride and jealousy are ugly, son. Even though he can be a charmer, I have to admit, he has become as ugly and dangerous as a bull nosed rattlesnake. I kept him right with me—gave him every opportunity. He can never say that I didn't give him a chance. What he has done was done before all the council of the great cloud of witnesses in heaven on the mount of assembly. His own actions of rebellion and wickedness and his plot against the settlers to enslave them on earth, rather than to serve them, and to then cause them to suffer eternally in the fiery torment of hell will be the evidence that condemns Satan."

"He was never going to be happy, Dad, unless he could take your place. I could see it, and so could you. And he was so jealous when you brought the settlers in. They didn't know. He really blindsided them. He could talk the fuzz off a peach!"

"Yes, he deceived them, but they knew the rule. It was their own decision. They will have to live—and die—with the consequences."

"But it's not just them—it's their children and all that follow after them! Their children's children. And he has a legal claim. It's the law. Now he owns them. All of them. I just don't understand why they believed his lies about you. We created them like us, in our own image, as our children!"

"We hadn't had much experience together. They—at least some of them—will get to know me and learn to trust me. And when they know me well enough, they won't fall for his lies anymore. They will know that I created them as my own children. To inherit this place. To be our family. Your brothers and sisters. To love and be loved. But he couldn't stand it. He added hate and violence to his sins—tricking them into sinning. He enslaved them to serve him instead of him serving them, and he intends for them to have an eternity of endless suffering with him."

"But now we have work to do first—to break the bondage for any who will turn from his rule and choose freedom and life. He didn't even consider that you would leave your place beside me and go live with them in the limitations of the flesh and show them the way, and it never dawned on him that you could or would pay the price to buy them back—your innocent blood for the penalty of sin. He believes he can stop you; and that no one will overcome, no one will love us enough to be faithful and loyal, but he is ignoring Job. There will be many like Job. Are you ready? You are the only one who can rescue them, if you are willing."

"I am willing, if it's the only way."

He nodded. "I love you, son. I wouldn't ask you if there was any other way."

Chapter ONE

The blackness was like a solid wall, and the noise was almost deafening, coming from all directions, bombarding my head like blows from a ball bat. I stood still and waited, hoping for something to change, to settle down. The stench in the place was as overpowering as the noise. My stomach churned and I turned in the darkness hoping to escape to some fresh air. Instead, I contributed to the stench with the partially digested breakfast from this morning. It didn't occur to me then what I was about to encounter. Maybe I would have skipped breakfast all together. Choices. We all make choices. Some turn out a whole lot better than others. The settlers have made some choices I wish they hadn't. But there is no going back now. Only through it. That was my choice. Sometimes I have misgivings, but the alternative is really not an option, in my mind. I've been watching. Something has to be done. There was no one else who could do it. Dad actually looked to see and could find no one. So it was me or nothing. So here I am. As my eyes adjusted to the light, or lack thereof, I began to make out the human forms of the settlers. They were crouched at tables, bent to eat with their hands out of large pots. They had no chairs to sit on. They pushed and shoved each other to get to the food. No one talked to each other, just screamed and bellowed curses as they competed for the gruel that ran and dripped off their hands if they weren't quick enough to slop it up with their mouth before it dripped on the table or back into the pot. A few seemed to dominate the area, cursing and threatening if someone was bold enough to try to scoop up some of the mess on the table to make it their own. But then the guards came in, beating everyone away from the tables with their night sticks. They ordered everyone to line up. It was time for them to go back to work. I had been assigned to this detail of slaves, my companions to be. All of a sudden, a scraggly old man stepped out of line and began preaching about a deliverer to come, some mighty warrior that their oral traditions had said would set them free. A guard dispatched the old man's head with one swift swing of his machete. He lay on the floor in two pieces. No one looked down or made a sound as they marched out the door.

I fell in line and noticed a young woman and a younger looking boy. To be truthful, one would have thought them to be ancients by their overall looks. Silent tears streamed down their faces, held only slightly above their hunched shoulders.

I knew the old man was not their grandfather as he appeared to be, but was rather her father, as he was also unduly aged as they were. No one spoke, only silently shuffled toward their destination. Many had not eaten at all when the food was provided, afraid to challenge the hoggish brutes who beat those who tried to get a share. So they returned to work with no food and no rest, weakened and listless, targets for the ire of the brutal guards who had leave to eliminate the weak, unproductive workers in any way their wicked minds could conceive. Cull the cattle. As we worked, one man injured himself, and cursed this hellhole. But I knew that as bad as this place was, it was not as bad as hell. There had been an indication of compassion, at least on the part of the boy and girl that one would assume were brother and sister, and the old man had spoken of hope. I knew hell has neither of these, compassion or hope. Not a tear from a loving heart, not a giggle from a baby, not the smell or color of a flower, not a drop of water to quench a raging thirst, not a hand lent to help, not the slightest hope of any kind— but only darkness, gnashing teeth, unbearable heat and sulfurous fire forever and ever and ever. No comfort and no kind word. Just the agonizing unbearable knowledge of forever. And the knowledge that it was a choice of their own making. Choices. How very important they are. I will keep an eye on choices while I am here. They will tell me much.

At the end of a long afternoon, we all filed back to the feeding room. Well, not all. Those of us who survived. Some didn't even approach the feeding table. They just sank in exhaustion onto the floor and propped themselves against the wall. I sat next to the girl and boy who were nearly brother and sister, by circumstances that cast their two families together. Now they alone remained of the two families. The girl's father, who had spoken words of hope and deliverance earlier that day, died for a faith he had in the promises of the ancients. I asked both of the youth on the floor beside me if they held the same beliefs. Both looked at each other, then at me, as if to say, we will choose to die, also, rather than deny our faith, and nodded their heads yes. I didn't see fear in their eyes, just a determined, matter of fact nod. I still had not asked their names. There didn't appear to be any camaraderie or socializing among the workers—this remnant of settlers into which I had been cast. In ways it is safer to be alone and unknown. Less likely for personal information to be betrayed or sold. And more protection for the heart against loss of relationships when people drop dead around you. But these kids had suffered a tremendous blow today. The only stability that had remained from their old life, whatever it was, was gone. Now it was just the two of them cast out on a sea of cruelty and terror and despair.

When I introduced myself and asked their names, they each pointed to the numbers on their arms. "What were your names before you were taken for the work crews?" I asked. The girl's eyes penetrated mine as she replied, "Lee," and the boy responded, "Roy." As they looked at each other, an almost undetectable smile seemed to be communicated through their eyes alone. A joke, a fond memory— a chosen identity to shield them from possible threats. I considered this a good sign of forethought and planning, of self-protection. Also a sign that a shred of humor lived. I knew how they ended up here and what their lives had been like before. But, I must go slowly if I want to penetrate the defenses and have them open up to me.

The brutes seemed to have finished eating what they wanted, so the rest of us rose and made our way to the table to stand and eat what was left. Lee and Roy paused for a moment before they reached out to take some gruel. It was a slight pause, hardly noticeable. A nod, and a shared look before they ate. My soul joined theirs in thanks, although I don't think they were aware of it. I was grateful for something in my stomach after suddenly emptying it this morning. I can't say I was "nose blind" yet, but the wretched smell was not impacting me quite so hard now. Everyone seemed to be too tired to be quite so noisy and aggressive, and my eyes had somewhat adjusted to the dim room that had a small light coming from somewhere around a corner that reflected dimly off of a wall in the back. I'm adjusting, but it sure ain't home. Home. How far away in so many ways. "*Dad, I am really going to need your help navigating this mission. It would be so easy to get off track—to forget the mission. You can't imagine the conditions, and the squalor, the suffering, and the twistedness of this place. Nothing like at the beginning. Guile's shadows drift among the settlers, stirring things up, whispering hatred and gossip among them. Planting ideas of violence, greed, and plots against each other. As I watch, the settlers seem oblivious to the shadows and their influence on them. They appear to be blind to the shadows, even though their presence and influence are quite obvious. I saw a shadow bend over and speak in one settler's ear, and immediately the settler began screaming at his wife and beating her. It didn't take much after that. Their children began fighting with each other, the bigger boy wailing on the smaller boy and twisting his arm almost out of the socket. Of course, he produced an ear piercing scream, which brought his father flying at him in a rage to 'Shut up!' as he grabbed the hysterical child and bashed his head against the wall. A guard looked in and then turned away as the child slumped to the floor dead. The mother's face was as passive and as dead looking as the child's, as she stared absently into nowhere. I sensed she had been dying in pieces, and as this event played out before her, her heart died, even though it still beat. The instigating shadow stood watching with a few others as the result of his work unfolded before them. Belly laughs accompanied high fives and fist bumps as the child was dragged unceremoniously by a leg out of the room.*

All of a sudden, another person appeared in the room—a shadow more formidable than the others. I recognized him immediately. He turned and looked at me, expressionless, for some time before turning to the other shadows. I saw him nod and look toward Lee and Roy, so I moved and sat down between them and the shadows. The shadows are clearly targeting them, so I must stay close.

The shadows are much changed from the beginning. They do resemble shadows; dull, without substance, not bright like they used to be. Their new name fits them well. Just shadows of what they used to be. Weak and ugly. Bullies. But there is an extreme anger and hatred with a maliciousness that exudes from every expression and action; an ugliness that obliterates the light and beauty that they had before they took up with Guile. Instead of even the slightest hint of repentance or apology for their traitorous, evil actions, all their energy is turned outward, bent on destruction—especially toward the settlers. Their jealousy and hatred for them nearly matches their jealousy and hatred for us. But, the settlers are much easier to torment than us, and they also know that it hurts us when they hurt the settlers. No loving parent wants to see their child in pain. So, they get to us through the settlers, and get to express their outrage that they are supposed to be ministering spirits to these weak, fleshly creatures who, because they were tricked into sin must now serve the shadows instead! You would think they would blame Guile, these Fallen Ones. He authored this whole thing and persuaded them with his poison tongue to fall in with him. I guess they do hate him, and each other, knowing that the dance is just about over. Their fate is sealed. They just don't know the how and when for sure, and they are literally fighting like hell, even though they know they can't win. But he still seems to have power over them. They made their choice, whom they would follow. And now they are facing the reality of their choice. But I guess misery does love company, and they are trying their best to make as many settlers suffer with them as they can. They were supposed to help the settlers and minister to them, but instead, Guile's jealousy and hatred of the settlers' place in your plan was contagious and infected about a third of the lights. And now their light is gone, swallowed up by the darkness, and they direct their hatred and jealousy in the most vicious way toward the settlers. How my heart aches for all the multitudes that will choose to follow the shadows into hell. Some of the settlers make jokes about it—if only they understood the truth, but they don't. Guile has them under his deluding influence. They think they can flip you off and exercise their rebellion and have their own kingdom in hell, raising hell, as they say. They have ears, but they are deaf. They have eyes, but they are blind. They have a mind, but no understanding, even when a man gives his life to tell them. They have a will, but they are bound as slaves to Guile who won them so many years ago when he deceived their ancestors. I have to admit, the settlers don't look much like they used to, either. Sometimes it's hard to even see a glimpse of our image in them. But to those who choose You, and submit themselves to the refining process, to be reconformed to Our image, they have such a glorious future! They will shed their corruptible and weak and mortal bodies, and receive their new perfect, incorruptible, immortal bodies! I get so excited when I think about it, Dad. I long for the day when we will bring them safely back home. And to see the amazement and joy on their faces! I know you want to free the settlers, and so do I, but will any even choose to come if they have the chance? Yes, some. Some will follow. I'll take any who will come with me. Any who are courageous enough to break with Guile. They don't have to be powerful, just courageous. And courage can live big, even in these small and young hearts. If they will follow, I will provide everything else they need to make it back home with me—back to you and freedom. And, yes, out of this hellish hole that they have learned to call home. But, Dad, I need you to send me a helper who can make his way around here without being detected by Guile and his gang.

Chapter TWO

Five years earlier

"Ivy, I need you to run to the store to get some milk. Here's some cash. Mr. Dale said he can't take checks anymore. The banks say it is too expensive to process the paper. That's all I have for now, I'll try to go to the bank and get some more tomorrow."

"Why don't we just get a card like everyone else? It is so much faster and easier, Mom. My friends just hold it up in front of the reader, and they are out of there."

"I know, honey. We can talk about it later when your father comes home."

———— ⟨⟨◉⟩⟩ ————

"Well, hello, Evan! What can I do for you today?"

" Just came to find out what the deal is. Lou said Ivy came in yesterday for some milk, and you told her you weren't going to be able to take her cash much longer."

"Yep. The card companies are making a good deal to retailers. They will install all the equipment and maintain it, but we have to agree to not take any other form of payment."

"But what about those of us who don't have a card and don't want one? I thought government currency was legal tender and people had to accept it."

"Almost everybody has already gone to the cards, Evan. There's just a handful of you dinosaurs left. People like the convenience and efficiency of the cards. You have a complete record of your transactions on line—makes your record keeping a whole lot simpler. You might as well get with the program, 'cause I hear the government is saying they could save a whole lot of taxpayer money if we just went to digital transactions. Besides the cost of printing money and making coins, it's a whole lot safer. They wouldn't have to worry about all kinds of criminal activity from counterfeiting to money laundering to tax evasion, if they could track all transactions digitally through one central bank. And I wouldn't have to worry about some drug head walking in here with a gun to rob what little cash I have. This little community can't afford our own law enforcement. It's got a lot of positives, from everything I've heard. What've you got against it, anyway, Evan?"

"Well, Dale, on the surface all that does sound pretty good. But I do have some serious reservations. First of all, what about the right to privacy? You know I pay my taxes and try to be a law-abiding citizen, Dale. I am not a criminal, nor do I intend to cheat the government, but I think it is a very unhealthy move in the wrong direction for a country like ours that is supposed to be free, to have the government watching all of our private affairs. Gives them too much power and information. Speaking of which—who else will have access to that information? You know as well as I do that all criminals don't carry guns and hold up stores. How many cyber hacks have we had over the years? Too many to count, and people have just resigned themselves that it is inevitable and shrug it off. Until it happens to them.

The good guys can't keep ahead of the crooks in that business. I don't want everything I have worked for to just disappear with the stroke of a key whether it is from a cyber criminal, the banks bailing out bad debts using other account holders' funds; or the government bailing themselves out to cover the national debt that is becoming unserviceable with their out of control spending. And that doesn't even touch the whole issue of the grid going down for any number of reasons. You know when they had that terrible hurricane that hit the islands? I heard a big part of the problems afterward with food and water and the like had to do with nobody being able to access the ATMs to buy what they needed, and had no communication, couldn't access their accounts or pay bills! No, thanks. I want money in my hands I can use. I don't want my survival dependent on an electronic system that someone else controls!"

"Boy, you're a real doomsdayer, aren't you, Evan? You know they say most of what we worry about never happens."

"It only takes one. Besides, Murphy's Law seems to be in play more often than not—if something can go wrong, it will. It is also called the second law of thermodynamics. Everything is going to break down, if not from wearing out, then because of greed for power and money. What's going to keep people from stealing my card, or even me losing it? The older I get, I can't seem to keep track of anything."

"Oh, you're just a young buck, Evan," laughed Dale. "Wait 'til you get my age, then you'll have something to complain about. Besides, they already have a plan for that. They have already run some trials on it."

"Oh, yeah? What's that?"

"I hear they have tiny microchips they can insert under the skin, and instead of holding your card or phone up to the reader, you just wave your hand under it or step up and it reads it under the skin on your forehead. And if you want extra security—it can read your eye, kind of like a finger print—biometrics, I think they call it."

Evan looked long and hard at Dale. He then turned and walked out of the store, calling over his shoulder, "Better read Daniel and Revelation in the Bible, Dale."

It really didn't take long after that. Everything with the government had to be done on line. Evan couldn't sign up for unemployment when the small factory in town closed. He couldn't apply for a new job without going online and scanning a mandatory government registration number. Since they closed most government offices to save money, the only way to do business with the government was online. They just announced that property taxes were now required to be paid online with an electronic debit from your bank account which required the mandatory registration number. Evan had so far skirted the issue as the government tried to sort out what to do with people who had no bank account and had not yet registered for their number. He knew time was running out. Most church officials were advocating compliance with the government mandate. They would lose their tax exempt status if they didn't, and their doors would close. Fewer and fewer people attended church, and most Bible preaching churches were struggling. Of course, those churches that had gotten in lockstep with the government were doing fine. Preaching from the government line, providing entertainment for all—something for everybody, and no mention of sin and the need for repentance. They called it tolerance, diversity, inclusiveness and love. To speak of sin and adhering to Biblical principles and calling people to repent and turn to

Jesus—the Way, the Truth and the Life—the only name under heaven by which people can be saved, they claimed was being intolerant, disrespectful, hating, and judging. It was illegal and could land you in jail for hate crimes. They took the pastors away and boarded up some of the churches. Enemies of the state. No one seemed to remember Bonheoffer and Solzhenitsyn. But Evan had read them... and now the riots and health issues around the world were pushing everyone toward a global government to control and manage all the chaos. Not much they can do about the natural disasters, he thought, but people need help to recover from them, and everyone had become dependent upon the government to do that. He expected a global government to be established soon. They were using a multipronged approach as the rationale to eliminate individual countries and establish a global government and economic system. In order to help control the pandemics that seemed to be ravaging the earth, they want a centralized health organization with mandatory immunizations and tracking devices, and enforcement power. In order to attempt to control climate change—they think much of their wisdom—they say they need enforceable world control of pollutants. And because of the collapse of national economies, they say we need to rebuild a world economy with no borders and a World Bank and centralized world economy, which they promise will be "fair" to everyone on earth. The new world government will own everything and give everyone what they need. Evan just shook his head as he thought about it. Communism pure and simple. And these leaders think they are so brilliant. They are like an obsessed Captain Ahab chasing the treacherous Moby Dick around the globe to their own destruction. They can't give the idea up, even though it has failed country after country around the world as an economic system, and plunged the people into dire poverty and slavery under its tyranny and despotism:

Eastern Europe, Cuba, Venezuela, China, —until they adopted a capitalistic economy, and the list goes on. Even though people under that system risk their lives and often die to flee from it, the utopian radicals seem to be able to sell their Kool-Aid to the weak minded, dependent and fearful. They don't understand that they are walking into a trap. It is a trap not set by humans, but by the antichrist using humans to set up his earthly kingdom to enslave and destroy mankind. It really isn't about politics and economic systems, but about the fulfillment of an age-old story played out in scripture and closing with the final book of Revelation. Evan had stopped walking and was staring out across a field as he contemplated these thoughts. He came to, shook his head, and began walking again toward home.

Evan opened the door. "John, Sarah! Come in. Didn't expect to see you so soon. What's happening?"

"We decided it was time. Things are changing fast, Evan."

"Where is Tony?"

"We told him to take his dog in the back yard and play for awhile."

"Ivy! We have company. Come down and say hi to the Parkers. Tony is in the back yard with his dog. You can take some drinks out for the two of you."

"Is Lou home?" asked Sarah.

"Not at the moment," replied Evan. "She should be back soon, though. A neighbor said she had some garden stuff for her. Here—let's go into the living room and sit down. Can I get you some water?"

"Sure. Sounds good," said John. "Have you heard the recent legislation that passed late last night?"

"No," replied Evan. "What's up?"

"Congress, as a formality, has officially disbanded as the last vestige of our sovereignty, and has declared that anyone who does not take the chip and swear loyalty to the new world order will not be able to do business at all. No groceries. No utilities. No gas. And if you don't pay your taxes using the prescribed chip, then you will lose your home. Won't be able to license your vehicle or pay for insurance—but it won't matter anyway, 'cause you won't be able to use it without gas. And after the pandemic, they have decided everyone has to prove they have had the vaccine, or they can't go out, anyway. And they just voted to join the global government so their peacekeeping force can control the rioters, and it will all be funded by the central government. They will assess everyone's digital account—whatever amount they decide—to fund the thing. No choice to opt out. They will redistribute money to feed the poor and open the borders, but of course, only those with chips and the permission of the central government can travel or will be relocated to have better access to resources. The people are buying it—worldwide—Europe, Africa, Asia, Australia, and now the whole western hemisphere. They have voted to turn their governments over to the central government in the hopes of stabilizing the world economy, controlling the violence, taking care of the immigrant issues, and supposedly mandating health requirements, including reducing the world population by whatever means they decide. Rumors have it that they have already sterilized populations in many undeveloped countries with additives to the vaccines. What most people don't understand is, it is a lie, a ruse, the vehicle for the antichrist to rise to power and enslave the world and enforce world worship of him."

Evan's shoulders slumped. "I knew this was coming, but I just kept hoping that someone would come to their senses and stop it. I knew better, but I wanted to believe this wouldn't happen. Have you had any contact with the Farm?"

"Yes. Just before we left. They still have room for us and you guys, too, if you have decided you want to go."

"Can't say it's my first choice, but I don't see we have options, because we are not getting the chip. So much for religious freedom." Evan shook his head in disbelief.

"This takes effect on Monday, Evan," said John. "So we don't have much time. We got all the gas we could. Emptied one can to get here. Do you still have a source where we can fill it?"

"I think so. Haven't been using much since I'm just working odd jobs mostly for barter. Been riding Ivy's bike most of the time," replied Evan. "We've put some coins away earlier before all this started snowballing. I think I can sell some to a dealer for cash to buy gas and food."

"It could be you have to find someone to get it for you in exchange for the coins. Someone who would prefer to have your coins and get rid of their cash. Cash isn't going to have much use after Monday, because everything will be digital after that," said John. "Bring every form of currency you have. The Farm has contacts and suppliers in the underground market that will deal and barter. They have been stockpiling essentials for a while, but I am sure they will deplete quickly as people start arriving."

Just then the front door opened and Louisa Thomas came through the door, looking expectantly for the passengers of the van out front. "John—Sarah! We weren't expecting you! What a nice surprise." As she looked from face to face, her countenance changed from delight to something like she was about to throw up.

Evan's heart sank. This was going to be so hard. Lou had practically refused to even think about this possibility playing out, let alone make plans for this reality. She had been raised a pre-tribber. The Bible says that God's followers will not experience the wrath of God, and Lou believed that meant the rapture of the believers would take place before the great tribulation and all the trials and suffering that would take place leading up to and during the reign of the anti-christ. Even though events have clearly been leading to this, it was simply unthinkable to Louisa that this could happen, being so contrary to her belief system. Jesus wouldn't possibly leave His followers here to go through this!

Evan read the events and predictions of scripture differently. Historically, he didn't see God protecting His people from trials and suffering. To the contrary, it seemed God used difficult times to prove and purify His people. To give them a testimony to a world of witnesses that His people would remain true to God and grow in faith in the living God. Hebrews chapter eleven talks of those who suffered and died for their faith, and others had miracles of deliverance, demonstrating the might and glory of God. He had His purposes in each and every case. In His wisdom and knowledge, in His power and sovereignty, He implemented His plan through His people. And because God is good, Evan trusted his Savior to do what was necessary and right. After all, earth is simply the training ground for heaven. Our stay here is temporary. God is going to burn up the current heavens and earth and create a new heaven and a new earth in which there will no longer be any evil or death or sorrow or pain. He believed that he would not experience the wrath of God, but that didn't mean the wrath that Satan wielded for the first part of his reign would not be felt by God's people. All those believers beheaded by Satan's reign are evidence of that fact. And God tells them to rest under the altar in heaven until the rest of their number is killed in the tribulation. The book of Daniel 12 clearly says in the end time many will be purged, purified, and refined, but the wicked will act wickedly; none of the wicked will understand, but those who have insight will understand. In verse 7, the angel tells Daniel that "as soon as they finish shattering the power of the holy people, all these events will be completed. Jesus promised persecution to His followers." But Lou just didn't buy it, and now here they were—faced with taking the mark of the beast, or not.

Most likely, they wouldn't survive even if they did run and drop off the grid. But Evan felt the responsibility to live as long as they could—to preach the way of salvation to any who would hear, and to help as many people as he possibly could through the holocaust that was coming and to be ready for the return of Jesus. He hoped to show the love of Jesus through the trials to come for as long as Jesus left him here. And if he should happen to live until that last of the trumpets sounds, he would have the magnificent reward of seeing the Lord come on the clouds with the mighty blast of that last trumpet and the shout of the archangel and see the dead in Christ rise from the dead and then follow them to meet Jesus in the air, as he feels his body changed in the twinkling of an eye into that imperishable eternal glorious body that is promised to all believers who remain faithful to the end. And even if he died before that trumpet sounds, Evan knew in the core of his being that it would be worth it all. Nothing could stop his death with the exception of Christ's return. And if he died before the return of Christ, then he wanted his death to count for Christ's kingdom—to show that, as Christ was faithful to those who love Him, that Evan would be faithful to Christ—to death. And all of God's promises would belong to Evan for eternity. Yes, it would be worth it all if he could just keep his eyes fixed not on this world and a temporary life here, but on Jesus, the author and completer of our faith. Evan knew, but what about his family? Could they understand Jim Elliot's statement: "He is no fool who gives up what he cannot keep, to gain what he cannot lose." God, please help Lou to understand.

As all of this was swirling through Evan's mind, John Parker explained to Lou about the new legislation that had just passed Congress and due to take effect the following Monday. Lou looked dumbstruck, and Sara moved toward her to wrap her arms around her. Lou shrank back from the embrace and slumped down into a chair.

"No. This can't be the mark. God wouldn't leave us here. We will just have to comply. That is what Christians are supposed to do. Obey the governing authorities, right," Lou stated to herself rather than to those standing around her. "This isn't it. This isn't the time. We will wait for God."

"Lou. We can't take the mark," said Evan. "We can stay here and refuse and become homeless and starve or get our heads chopped off immediately, or we can go with John and Sarah while we still can. It isn't like we don't know what's coming. It is all written in scripture. The lessons of the Jews who wouldn't leave Germany before WWII, should instruct us, Louisa. I think we should try to stay alive as long as we can. Lou, I know it's hard for you to believe, but contrary to what you believe, THIS IS IT. We have an eternal choice to make—Heaven or hell. There is only one sane choice. Obey Jesus."

"Oh, you and your obsession with Revelation! Can't you think about anything else? There is more to life and to Christianity than that one book of the Bible! The new preacher said it was not to be taken literally—it's just metaphors and allegory. The important thing is to try to live good lives. Why can't you just accept that?"

"Lou, I can't because we're living it—we're living Revelation. It was written for us—those who are living in these times so we know what to expect, what to do—and what NOT to do. Lou, can't you see? We just can't take the mark."

"I can't live with this anymore, Evan. You are on the verge of insanity and I am not going to be swallowed up in this. You go wherever you want, but I am not going with you. I have been thinking of going to visit my parents, and it looks like there is no better time. When you come to your senses and come home, we can make an appointment for counseling for you. I think you need that cult brainwashing therapy. I'll ask the pastor if he knows someone who can help."

"Lou—,"

"No, Evan! I'm done with this," interrupted Louisa as she marched out of the room.

The remaining three in the room exchanged looks. John raised both his eyebrows about as high as he could raise them, "Well, Evan, what are you going to do?" The urgency of time pressured John to press for a decision.

"My decision is already made," replied Evan. "Lou and I have been over this many times. She's never come down to a refusal before. Probably thought nothing would come of it—just ride it out, I suppose. But I can see she has thought it out, and has made her own decision, too. She isn't going to change her mind. At least, not yet. Perhaps after things get worse, she will see more clearly and I can return for her."

"Not if she has taken the mark, Evan," replied John. "Then she will be under the deluding influence. There will be no turning back for her."

At that, Evan bounded up the stairs to their bedroom where Lou was packing a bag. "Lou, please reconsider. Come with us and if you are right and nothing comes of this, then I will bring you home. Please. I'm begging you. Please! I love you. Don't leave. Please."

"If you love me, you could stay here," replied Louisa. "But I already know the answer to that. You must love God more than me—whole heart, mind, soul, and strength, right? Well, what about loving me? God says husbands, love your wives, too, you know! Well, I'm tired of being second place to your whacko theology! And I am furious that you have brainwashed and indoctrinated our daughter. I can't take her to my parents, but I will fight you for her. I am determined she will have a normal life."

"Lou, I do love you. Please always remember that. I can't love you well enough in my natural man. I am weak, and selfish, and unable to love you the way you deserve and need without the spirit of God in me, teaching me how to love beyond myself. I know it doesn't feel like that right now, but because I love you, I care about your eternity as well as whatever life we have left on this earth. I care not only about your wishes and making a life for you here, but I can't bear the thought of you making choices that will separate you from God and put you in hell—unending torment forever! I am trying to protect you and love you! Please, Lou, hear my heart!"

"I hear your heart, alright. I hear you judging me just because I don't believe your crazy theology. Your sense of superiority disgusts and infuriates me! Now get out of my way. I am going to tell Ivy goodbye and that I will be fetching her to come home when school starts again."

Ivy found Tony and his dog in the back yard. As she handed him a glass of water, she asked, "What's his name again?"

"Leroy," he responded.

"Oh, yea, I forgot," replied Ivy. "Is he smart?"

"My mom says he's dumb like a fox. He doesn't really do tricks, or anything. But, Ivy, it's weird, he always knows what's going on. He has this sense. Sometimes when this kid on my block tries to grab my lunch on the way to school, or is coming at me saying he is going to teach me some respect or some other dough head thing, Leroy just shows up, grabs my lunch and runs across the street with it to wait for me, or walks right between him and me like a football blocker. People say Leroy is dumb, but if he is, I don't know how he always has my back."

"Hmm," was all Ivy said, skepticism in her manner. All of a sudden she lunged at Tony, but before she made contact, Leroy took her out and was standing over her wagging his tail as she gasped for breath, flat on the ground.

"Wow, that's amazing!" laughed Ivy. "Well, Leroy, I'm a believer," she said as she got up off the ground.

"Are you?" asked Tony.

"Well, he just convinced me!" said Ivy.

"No, I mean, are you a believer? You know why we're here, don't you?" asked Tony.

"What do you mean? Why do you usually come? Just to visit or pray or talk, I guess," replied Ivy.

"Not this time. Time to pray and talk is over. Dad read out of Daniel 11 where it says the anti-Christ will deceive unbelievers with smooth words and turn people away from God, but that people who know their God will be strong and take action. And that they have insight and will give understanding to many. But that many will die in standing for God. But Dad said Revelation 14—I can't remember the verse—says that those who stay true to God and die for Him will have a special blessing. I'm kind of scared, Ivy. Dad says if we think about it wrong, it can seem scary, but we have to keep remembering Jesus, keep our eyes fixed on Him and what He went through for us, and that God is in control and He will make it all work out for good because it's all part of His plan. Even if we die, we will live. Forever with God in the new heaven and new earth. So Dad said we must take courage and take action to try to help people understand what is going on. Because if they don't and take the mark of the Beast, they will suffer in hell forever. So we are headed to the Farm, and stopped by to pick you guys up if you decide to go with us. Mom and Dad didn't call because they figured all the phones are monitored. I don't know where it is. The directions are secret. Everyone is assigned to the Farm site that is closest to them. The government passed some laws last night that say everyone has to get a mark on their hand or forehead or they can't do any business with the government or buy and sell. No more cash. Everyone has to comply by Monday."

Ivy stood motionless for several seconds. "Dad said this was coming, and I believed it, but it was kind of like a fairy tale in some ways, you know? Something we read in the Bible, and believed because it was the Bible, but also didn't seem real, like it really wouldn't happen, even though things have been happening and Dad said we have to be ready. Today? Right now?" said Ivy with building agitation in her voice as she ran toward the house.

Just then her mother rounded the corner of the house and called to Ivy. "Mom, is it true? Are we going to the Farm? Today?" asked Ivy.

Louisa took her daughter's hands in hers. "I think it's just a scare, honey. Your dad thinks you should go, but I am sure you will be back when school begins next month. I am going to see your grandparents until then, and I will come get you. It'll all work out fine in time. Don't worry. We will be together again in a few weeks."

"Mom, are you sure? Why aren't you coming with us? What's happening?" Ivy wept as her mom took her in her arms and hugged her good-bye. Shaken, Ivy watched as her mom drove away as she slowly climbed the steps to the house feeling her world reeling in slow motion around her, unable to take it all in. Her dad joined her on the step and put his arm around her. Together, they watched Louisa drive away.

Louisa watched her husband and daughter in the rear view mirror until they were out of sight. Tears streamed down her cheeks. *What just happened? What did she just do? She just left the two people she loved most in the world. But she couldn't let Evan's crazy theology turn their world upside down, dragging them away to who knows where to live in some weirdo compound called The Farm. It struck Lou that she didn't even know where they were going. That was top secret, and although within their group, they talked freely about the Farm, they never disclosed where it was. The question crossed her mind that she may not be able to contact them or find them if this didn't go away in a month. Why didn't she ask questions? Because you were so angry you didn't think rationally. Angry and scared. Scared spitless. Yes, that's what's really driving you, girl, isn't it? You always have comforted yourself that the rapture would take you out before you will show yourself to be a weak coward. If Evan is right, then you're in trouble. It is easier to deny than face the possibility that you may have to suffer persecution. You have done the mental equivalent of covering your ears and shouting la la la whenever Evan brought up scriptures that showed Christians must suffer and be persecuted for the name of Jesus Christ. Hebrews 11 was about the Old Testament, you argued. But Daniel 11 and 12 written about the end times was harder to argue with. In fact, Evan had pointed out that more Christians had been martyred in the past hundred and fifty years than all the rest of the martyrs combined since Jesus. It actually says that in the end times those who have insight will suffer terrible things and death to refine, purge, and make them pure until the end comes. Well, God, I don't know if I can take that! I don't want to be one of the saints under the altar who had their heads chopped off in the tribulation, waiting for the rest who still needed to complete the number of martyrs. I can't bear the thought of Ivy... NO! my parents, my church, I believed that you would protect us from that. I thought you loved us and would protect us!* Louisa was crying so hard now that it was hard to see out the windshield. Then she realized it was raining—coming down hard now. *What about the Christians all over the world who have been dying for Christ, Evan had argued. I need to go back*—as Louisa swung into a U turn, all she heard was a deafening crash.

Chapter THREE

W hen they arrived, few rooms were left. In order to accommodate as many people as possible, both families were put in one room—the Parkers in a double bed and the other three in two bunks. Everyone shared a public space, and ate meals in a communal dining room prepared in a kitchen that was not overly large or well equipped, but adequate. There were lots of daily chores that needed done, and a very large garden to tend as well as a milk cow and lots of chickens to care for. A twenty-four hour prayer vigil was established in rotating shifts in the chapel. Some people called it the "war room," but regardless of what it was called, it was a determination of these believers to call upon the God in whom they had put their trust to lead them in the days to come, to make them effective witnesses, to deliver the world from the deep darkness that was smothering it, and to bring salvation to as many people as possible while there was still time. They confessed their sins to one another and of their nation. They clung to 2 Chronicles 7:14 and humbled themselves and prayed and sought God's face, and turned from their wicked ways, so that God might heal their land, indeed, the world. For they received news that the U.S. economy had crumbled along with the rest of the nations', and the world was in such a turmoil that all the nations agreed that it would take a unified government and economic system as well as a peace-keeping force to manage all the rioting and ensure protection of the environment. All nations ceded their sovereignty to the one world government, accepted a completely digital economy that was to be monitored by the world banking system, and agreed to an international army to ensure the peace. Anyone who did not comply was killed immediately, or if able-bodied, was sentenced to be re-educated in the work camps. Communication with the other sister Farms was no longer possible or safe. Some of them had been discovered by satellite and were obliterated by drones. Some had been invaded by troops and killed or captured. Helping those in need around them posed risks, to be sure, but many people had come to know Jesus Christ and received eternal life. But Ivy felt like the walking dead. What had happened to her world? What happened to her mom? When would the troops come here?

"Ivy?" said Evan.

"Hmmm?" replied Ivy as she looked up from her book. They were on their break, and Ivy lost herself in a book.

"Can we talk?" asked her father. "I feel like I've lost touch with you. I need to know what's in your heart, what you've been thinking about?"

"I try not to think. There doesn't seem to be any answers. What's going to happen to us? Where is Mom? What's happened to her? How long will we be in this constricted place? Worse yet, how long until they come to take us, too? This waiting with no answers is just unbearable!"

"I know it's hard, sweetheart. And they may come for us. I don't know what God's will is when it comes to that. I don't know if we will be some of those who will remain alive to see His coming, or not, or if we will be killed for a short time before we are resurrected from the dead and rise to meet Him in the air. But we do know there is a total time frame of seven years, and then it will be over. Christ will return and we will be safe with Him. It is just very important that we don't give up. We must keep loving and serving Jesus until He comes back for us."

Ivy looked at Evan full in the face, her eyes searching the depths of her father's eyes. "Do you really believe that, Daddy?"

"With all my heart, Ivy," replied Evan. "What about you, Ivy? What do you believe?"

"I used to believe. But it was different. It just seemed like it was what I was told in Sunday school and church, and what you and Mom taught me, and it was like believing that the world was round, or believing that two plus two equaled four. It was what everyone believed and of course, I believed it too. But it is different now. There's more to it. Our whole life has changed because of what we believe. I don't know what to think—or if I believe THIS! What this is NOW."

Evan took Ivy in his arms and she cradled her head against his neck. "I think my little girl is growing up! I guess you're getting pretty big to fit on my lap," chuckled Evan.

Ivy smiled a little smile, "You know I'm going to be fifteen, Dad."

"Holy Moley!" Evan declared with feigned surprise. "I guess that will be pretty soon, too. Can't believe we have been here six months."

"It seems like six years, Dad."

"Yes, in some ways it does, doesn't it?" replied Evan. "You know, it seems like things are letting up a little, calming down. There aren't as many raids on the Farms as in the beginning, not as much turmoil. The new world leader seems to be focusing on gathering support, building the temple in Jerusalem, pacifying people. It is amazing how exactly it is fitting into what the Bible says. What we believed is true, Ivy. Will you look at the scriptures with me again? You can read it for yourself and decide," said Evan as he picked her Bible up off the end of the bed.

"Sure. I have been trying to read it, but it's hard to concentrate, and even if I do, it's hard to understand sometimes."

"Ok," said Evan. "God gave His words to us so we can understand and know Him. He's a person. Jesus is alive. He went back to heaven to wait for the appointed time for Him to come and end evil and establish His eternal kingdom with His people. He has sent His Holy Spirit to teach us and be with us until He returns. One of the things the Holy Spirit does is help us understand God's Word. So let's ask Him to do that now while we read together."

After Evan and Ivy prayed for God to open their hearts and minds as they read, Evan said, "I don't want to begin right away in Revelation. First, I want to go to the end of Matthew chapter 28 and then to the first chapter of Acts so you can see the beginning of the rest of God's plan that Jesus lays out for His disciples to do before He comes back again."

"So that is what we are trying to do here at the Farm, Ivy," said Evan when they finished those passages. We are trying to reach people with the truth of the gospel as we help them, to make disciples and bring them into eternal life in God's kingdom. Now let's read in the book of Matthew chapter twenty-four. Here the disciples ask Jesus about when will He set up His kingdom, and He gives them signs, but says of the exact day or hour, only the heavenly Father knows. But then He warns them that they must be alert and ready for Christ's return—don't be slack and disobedient like the servant who doesn't do what he is supposed to be doing while his master is gone and suffers the punishment Jesus describes."

When they finished that chapter, Evan asked Ivy, "What are some things that stand out to you in this chapter, Ivy?"

"Well, there will be false prophets trying to mislead people."

"Yes. Anything else?" asked Evan.

"Well, I don't like this part that says we will be delivered to tribulation and that they will kill us and everyone will hate us because we believe in Jesus, and that many will stop believing in Jesus and will betray the people who do. That just doesn't seem right, Dad. Why would God let that happen?"

"That's a fair question, Ivy," replied Evan, "and I want to give you a good answer to that. I will explain it to the extent that I understand it. But can we talk about that another time so we can finish this discussion right now, about how to understand these times we are living in?"

"Sure," nodded Ivy.

"Good. So getting back to Matthew 24, what else stands out to you?"

"Well, when Jesus comes back, it won't be a small thing, or a secret—it will be like the whole sky is lit up with lightning when He comes and everyone will know it. And it will be after the tribulation is over and at that time He will send out His angels to gather up the elect, but the tribes of the earth will mourn when they see Him coming. Who's the elect and who are the tribes?" asked Ivy.

"The Bible refers to the elect as those who belong to God—those who love Him and have received salvation," replied Evan. "And the tribes of the earth are also people referred to as the nations—those who are not followers of Christ. Anything else?"

"I guess not."

"So—let's go to second Thessalonians chapter two. The apostle Paul is writing a letter to the Thessalonians and wants to clarify some things for them. Chapter two begins with Paul saying he wants to talk about the coming of the Lord Jesus Christ and our gathering together to Him. Sometimes people call this the rapture. He had written his first letter to the Thessalonians about this event starting in chapter four, verse 13. He was talking about people who had already died in Christ, and what was going to happen to them, because apparently some people were grieved that their loved ones weren't alive for the coming of Christ. He told them that when Jesus comes back, with a shout, with the voice of the archangel and the last trumpet of God, that the dead in Christ will actually be resurrected first. Then we who are alive and remain at Christ's coming will be caught up together with them in the clouds to meet the Lord in the air, and then would always be with the Lord. But apparently there was some confusion about that and some people had said that Jesus had already returned and the rapture, or gathering to Christ had already taken place. People were upset, thinking they had missed the boat, so to speak. Paul wrote—see in verse three?—that he didn't want them to be deceived and that it was not going to happen until the falling away from faith came first and the man of lawlessness, or the anti-Christ, is revealed and declares himself to be God, and takes his seat in the temple in Jerusalem to be worshipped. Then, and only then, will the rapture and return of Jesus take place, Paul said."

"Then why does Mom believe Christians will be raptured before the Tribulation?" asked Ivy.

"Mostly because that is what she has been taught—kind of like you were saying about you believed because that is what you were told. Also, I think it is what we want to believe—that we won't have to go through persecution and suffering," said Evan.

"It is a lot easier to believe. And if it turns out as Mom believes, then, hey, that would be great! But if not, then I think it is better to be prepared so Satan doesn't blindside us, and we become some of those many that the Bible says will fall away from faith in Jesus in the end times. The New Testament is full of warnings to the followers of Jesus to be alert and be ready. Jesus has a lot to say in Matthew 10 about being betrayed by people who we wouldn't expect, and says in Matthew 10:22, '... it is the one who has endured to the end who will be saved.' He says the same things in many other places, especially in Revelation to the churches. But I don't believe Jesus was only speaking to the first century church. He doesn't have one standard for them and a different standard for us. In fact, many of the prophecies quoted are from the Old Testament and state they are specifically about the end of time right before the return of Christ—so the prophecies were for back then, the first century church, and for those living in the end times."

"So what does Revelation say about it?" asked Ivy.

"To be honest, it is more difficult to sort out, because no one is sure exactly how to interpret it. We are not sure that it is written chronologically, that one event follows the other in sequence. It also is filled with similes and metaphors, and some figurative language because the writer, the apostle John, didn't have words to describe what he saw. Some people say it isn't to be taken literally, or we cannot understand it, but that is contrary to John's purpose as he writes in the first three verses, 'The Revelation of Jesus Christ, which God gave Him to show to His bond-servants, the things which must soon take place; and He sent and communicated by His angel to His bond-servant John, who testified to the word of God and to the testimony of Jesus Christ, to all that he saw. Blessed is he who reads and those who hear the words of the prophecy, and heed the things which are written in it; for the time is near.' I don't think it is to confuse us. We are to read it, understand it, and heed it. We should read it like the rest of the Bible—straightforward—but for instance, if John writes that something is "like" something, we know that is a simile, a comparison to something else. But there is a real object he is trying to describe. It isn't fiction. But there are some places where we can see if we can know if we are living in the end times, and where approximately in the time frame we are, and if we can expect the rapture to take us out prior to the tribulation. Here are some passages you can study on your own, but our break time is over. I do want to discuss them with you later, though." He handed her a list: Rev. 6:9-17; 7:1-3; 7:9-17; 8:1; 9:1-4; 13:1-7-18 (the beast, 42 months, wars with saints, not buy or sell). I am not sure when exactly the rapture takes place in relation to the seven years of tribulation, but these scriptures indicate to me that followers of Christ are still here quite some time into the tribulation. I want to hear what your take on these passages is, Ivy."

"Ok. I will try to read them tonight, Dad."

"Ivy, you mean the world to me. I am so sorry your mother didn't come with us, and I know you miss her. I pray every day that she will somehow find her way here. I miss her, too."

With tears in her eyes, Ivy said, "I pray for her every day, too, Dad."

They hugged and walked to the kitchen to help prepare dinner.

The leadership team was called together to deal with some issues that had arisen. Some thought this was a good time to send out scouts. Government attention seemed to be focused elsewhere than on the "NCC's" –non-compliant criminals, as those who did not take the mark were called. The team needed to find sources who would take gold for supplies. They were still ok, but it was winter now and the gardens weren't producing. The food supplies would diminish fast. And they needed a source for fuel. Mr. Wright was reluctant to continue supplying them, afraid that the authorities would find out. He was going to have to give an account of his stocks, and then they would be monitoring his volume against his income. If his stocks became depleted, without showing income from sales through the bank, someone would be showing up at his door to find out why. He had been willing to take gold, when he could hide it from the bank, but now the system would be monitoring his volume against his transactions. Too risky, he said. The Farm leadership was careful to limit fuel use, and having solar to heat water and a wind turbine to pump it and wood for heat, they could manage, but they didn't have any transportation besides a few bikes and a team of horses and a wagon if they didn't have fuel for Parker's van. They didn't know if any supplies were left in any of the sister Farms that had been raided. Getting to them to find out would be really risky. The leadership team decided to hold off awhile and see if it stayed quiet. They figured they had some time— maybe up to three years or so before the temple was finished and the world leader took his seat in it, declaring himself to be God and demanding to be worshipped. Maybe Jesus would come back for His followers before then, but maybe not. At any rate, their job was to reach as many people as possible before the end. There were still people who were turning to Christ, although it was at great risk that the followers shared their beliefs. So far, no one on this Farm had been betrayed, but many of the Farms had suffered great loss for sharing the truth and helping people. Spies—or as the book of Daniel calls them, hypocrites, actors— had infiltrated some of the Farms and exposed them. Even so,

God was doing marvelous things in answering prayer for people, and they were seeking this God who was demonstrating His great and mighty love for them. Many stories had been told of how God had helped in the earlier days when He would blind the eyes of border guards to the bibles that were being smuggled into communist countries. Similar things were happening now and they felt the hand of God protecting them. But either way, they were ready to live or die for Christ, knowing that as Jim Elliot had summed up the words of Christ, "He is no fool who gives up what he cannot keep, to gain what he cannot lose." Jesus said that His followers would be hated and persecuted even to death for following Him. That had taken place through the centuries as His followers stood for Jesus in their cultures. And whether it was local or worldwide persecution, they had chosen to take their stand and consider it an honor to suffer for Christ. They believed in the promise of their resurrection to eternal life, and these temporary sufferings could not compare to the glory of their sure hope in Jesus Christ and life in Him. But they felt they had work to do until they died or Jesus returned. That work was to rescue as many people from the clutches of Satan and an eternity in hell as they could. So they decided to pray for guidance about when they would or even should venture out.

God seemed to be using this time to be refining them within the Farm campus. Each person arrived with their own unique personality, strengths, and weaknesses, each in their own point of development in their Christian walk and maturity. Each had their own understanding of the Word and its application to their life, or lack thereof. The circumstances of confined spaces, limited resources, demands of work and cooperation that many were not accustomed to, really was a refining fire and discipline for most of them. The simplest things that most of them had taken for granted in America, like food and drink, became a stumbling block to many. Food for most Americans, even for the poor, was more a matter of convenience and preference, not an urgent necessity to keep their bodies alive. They didn't have to look to the natural environment for what was growing to sustain their bodies from day to day. The question was more often "to cook or not to cook?" If not, then where will I drive through, carry out, or will we go sit down and have someone cook for us? The question was, "What sounds good?" or "What am I in the mood for tonight?" The question was seldom, "What is available?" And certainly not the same thing we've had for the past three days for lunch. So food became one of the most difficult adaptations the residents of the Farm had to make. They complained about plain oatmeal every day for breakfast. They were agitated without their coffee and soda, and bored out of their minds with plain water for the only beverage. They snapped at one another, short tempered and irritable. Some didn't like squash, others didn't like fish. Others wanted larger portions or more meat. Suddenly, what they had taken for granted became center focus and a point of grumbling and contention—and theft.

Some had been accustomed to physical labor and the sweat of their brow as their means of supplying for their livelihood. Others had the foresight as they contemplated the approaching trials, to condition their bodies and discipline themselves to training their minds and bodies to endure hardship and develop mental toughness. Others had lived their lives with as much ease, pampering and comfort that they could afford. When life became difficult, neither their bodies, nor minds, nor expectations, nor attitudes were prepared. Others resented the "weak ones" for expecting others to take up their slack and having an expectation to be served. After all, they were not accustomed to getting dirty and sweating with no air conditioning and certainly couldn't ruin their nails! And the withdrawal from technology produced high anxiety. Of course, the inability to obtain all the prescription and over the counter drugs that the residents were accustomed to for coping with the trials of life presented its own issues. The Farm became a boiling pot of purification and refinement. There was much dross that God needed to bring to the surface to be skimmed off so true love and forgiveness and patience and kindness could be practiced.

Ivy and Tony were no exception. Their bickering was stretching their parents to the limits and left them at a loss as to how to deal with it.

"I think I hate him, Dad," said Ivy of Tony after an especially bitter quarrel.

Evan took Ivy by the hand, "Come walk with me, Ivy." They walked down to the pond and sat on some benches by the edge of the water, where the raised catfish came swimming up, expecting to get some food pellets tossed to them. "You know, we have choices here, Ivy. And I would like to explore those choices with you and what they mean to us, to others around us, and especially to Jesus."

Ivy sat silently as her father spoke. The silence hung between them, Evan waiting for her reply. She was reluctant, because she knew where this was going and she was still really mad at that annoying thorn in her flesh, and really wasn't ready to give up her anger—not yet. It felt good to vent and hold Tony hostage to her anger. She was mad, mad at him, mad at these circumstances they had to live in, and if she was honest, mad at her dad for turning her life upside down, even though she believed he was right, and mad at her mom for not coming with them, even though she missed her terribly and was scared out of her mind for her. So scared she tried to not even think about her, but the more she tried to block it out, the more it consumed her. Her mind felt like a hamster running endlessly on a wheel in its cage. The same thoughts over and over, but never an answer. Sometimes she thought she would go out of her freaking mind. No, she didn't want to talk about it. It seemed so hopeless, and it made her chest and head hurt. She didn't have the energy to drag herself up that mountain. So she just sat there, silent.

Evan sensed his daughter's anger and despair, but was at a loss at how to reach her. "God, please help me help Ivy. I don't know what to do or say. Please reach her heart and help her find her way to You in this," Evan silently prayed as he sat by his daughter watching the fish darting under the surface of the water. "What are you thinking, sweetie?" asked Evan, taking her hand in his.

Her first impulse was to pull it away, but there was warmth and comfort in his large hand as it encompassed hers, something strong when she felt so lost. So she kept it there in his hand. She didn't answer right away. "I don't know what to think, Dad," she finally replied. "It hurts to think. And then I get sad, so sad I think my heart is being squeezed so hard it will surely burst, but there isn't even a place I can cry in private here. And then I get so mad, I just want to scream my lungs out! But I can't do that, either. So I guess it's just easy to take it out on Tony." Then she snorted, "Except for Leroy. Bodyguard dog. Dumb dog that knows everything dog." They both chuckled at that.

Evan pulled her to his side. "Ivy, I am so, so sorry you hurt. If I believed there was any other way, I would do it. Time has gotten by with all the work there is to do and we haven't really spent much time talking about those scriptures I asked you to read. Have you finished those yet?" She nodded. "So what is your take on those?" he asked.

"I think you are right, Dad. It says there are believers still here at least part of the time during the reign of the beast. Because the rapture can't take place before the beast is revealed. They are being killed for being faithful to Jesus. At times they get some protection from the suffering inflicted on the earth, but sometimes they are the target. I do know we can't take the mark, and we are seeing the beast ruling the earth and rebuilding the temple. I think it has begun. Whether I like it or not, we are in it. But then, Dad, I keep thinking about Mom! Where is she? What is happening to her? I am so scared for her!"

"Ivy, I'm not going to tell you that I know the answer when I don't. Or that I'm not scared, too, when there are times that my heart aches with fear for her. But I do know this, that God says we are to put our faith and trust in Him, and that we are to take courage and not fear—that Satan can use fear as a tool against us. I also know that God says to pray and diligently seek Him and not give up and keep praying. So even though I can't DO much, I can always pray and ask the all powerful God to do what I am unable to do. He knows where she is, and is watching over her right now. I love your mother more than life itself, Ivy. But I can't make decisions for her. But I can pray for her always and ask God to protect her from the influence of the beast, to keep her safe and to make sure she is with Him and us in heaven when this is all over. And I can pray knowing that it is His will. Jesus came for that very purpose, so people can be saved. He didn't want to die for nothing—He wants us to believe, repent and be saved. He says He is not willing that any should perish, but that all would be saved from eternal destruction. So even if we die in this body, we will have eternal life in Him. That's what I can do—pray, and that isn't some trite little hopeful, wishful thinking, Ivy. It is calling to the living God and all the powers of heaven to rescue your mom from the powers of hell that have already been defeated at the cross. Your mom believes that, Ivy. I am trusting God to rescue her from the schemes of the devil.

Will you turn your worry into prayers, Ivy, and join me with faith believing for your mom?"

"Every day, Dad," replied Ivy. Together they bowed their heads before the throne of grace for their wife and mother.

Chapter FOUR

"Mr. and Mrs. Johnson. Thank you for coming in today."

"Please call us Jim and Clara, Doctor," replied Jim.

"Of course," returned the Doctor. "I have asked to see you about the progress of your daughter, Louisa Thomas. I have to be honest, I never expected her to make it. The fact that she lived through that wreck with the semi truck is unexplainable. And it's just as amazing that she is recovering from the massive injuries she sustained. She has a long way to go, but you need to be thinking about convalescent care as soon as she no longer needs daily medical care and can get to the toilet—maybe even with a little help. She can do rehab on an outpatient basis. There is the issue of the chip that will eventually have to be addressed. I see no need to press that until she is stronger and is not so heavily sedated with pain medication, because a fully cognizant decision is required."

"Yes, thank you, Doctor," replied the Johnson's. "When she is well enough, we're sure she will comply. We have already decided she will stay with us, close to her medical facilities." They didn't mention that her husband and daughter had disappeared and not been heard from since the accident. No need to raise embarrassment and suspicion. Everyone had learned it is best to be as invisible as possible. Although no one was invisible to the eyes of

5G and satellites. Some of the infrastructure had been destroyed by the bombings, but along with the rebuilding of the temple in Jerusalem, one primary focus of this New World Order and the Regime ruled by the man called the Beast, was to build out the network as fast as possible. The Beast Man and his machine intricately enmeshed, creating an electronic web encircling the planet, to monitor every neighborhood, every financial transaction, every communication, every person at nearly real time speed. The world's resources and manpower were focused on this effort. For the sake of peace and safety, to rid the planet of crime and violence, no one questioned the plan or authority, but rather committed themselves to the cause for the good of all. If anyone disagreed, they quietly disappeared into the "re-education camps," never to be seen again, or to emerge Compliant.

"That has got to be one of the scroungiest dogs I have ever seen," commented Ivy as she watched Tony and the dog try to out maneuver each other in a game of tag.

"But he's a good dog. Looks ain't everything, as they say. He likes me and he's loyal and defends me. More than I can say for some people."

Ivy thought a bit before she spoke. "Dad's been talking to me about how we need to practice love and forgiveness in our everyday living if we are going to be prepared for the hard big things when they come."

"You mean what Pastor spoke about in the meeting yesterday," replied Tony.

"Yes," nodded Ivy. "We are supposed to love and cherish each other and when we get on each other's nerves, we are supposed to forgive each other. Jesus said our love for one another is supposed to demonstrate that we are His disciples. That is what Dad has been trying to get through to me, but I didn't want to hear it. And I guess from what Pastor said, I'm not the only one."

"Even among the grown-ups," said Tony. "I've heard some nasty things being said."

"Dad says we're all in process, all at different places in our spiritual development, so we need to be patient and forgiving and kind. It was easy to sing songs about the fruits of the Spirit, but this is something else—actually trying to practice them," replied Ivy. "But in the service yesterday when Pastor spoke and asked us to quietly pray and ask God to speak to our hearts, I really felt God did speak to me."

"What did He say?" asked Tony.

"You know it wasn't out loud—but somewhere in my head and heart I knew I needed to treat you better, and to ask you to forgive me. I know I've been mean. I'm sorry. Will you forgive me?" asked Ivy.

"Sure. If you will forgive me," replied Tony.

"For what?" asked Ivy as she looked into Tony's face.

"I know how to get you going—how to irritate you and needle you to get you to lose your temper. Even though you are older and bigger than me and act superior to me, it was a way I could control you and get you in trouble."

"You little rat!" exclaimed Ivy. After a pause, she replied, "I guess we both need forgiveness. That's kind of what God was showing me yesterday. We are all sinners and need to forgive each other if we want Him to forgive us. That's why He died. And if we won't forgive others who He died for, then we are like trying to defeat His purpose, like standing against Him. Like Satan—standing on Satan's team accusing our brethren in our hearts. And then Satan uses that against us to accuse us, and our own unforgiveness eats at us, spoiling our hearts and our love and our peace. That was what God helped me understand."

"So what now?" asked Tony.

"Well," replied Ivy, "I think we should make a pact. We agree to be on the same team. We aren't against each other. Jesus is our captain and calls the shots. We try to help each other be the best player we can be, instead of competing against each other. Satan is our enemy who is literally trying to destroy us. This is no game. This is life and death for us and everyone else. He is killing us off. But even if we die, we will win, because Jesus has already defeated Satan when He died on the cross for us. And He wants us to be ready to die for each other—to be like Him, to have the kind of love He had for us."

"Sounds good," replied Tony. "I just don't know if I can do it. I'm sure I will mess up."

"Me, too. But that is when we put patience and forgiveness into practice. Like Dad says, we need to practice and practice and practice until the ways of Jesus become ingrained in us. And we can help each other do that by speaking the truth in love. Dad says we need to give permission to each other to speak the truth in love."

"You mean like when you are acting superior to me, instead of getting mad and trying to get back by needling you, I just say, 'Hey, Ivy, you're acting like a jerk. Knock it off?'"

"Don't forget the 'in love,' part, doofus, otherwise you'd just be starting a fight again."

"So you want me to say, 'In love, Ivy, you're acting like a jerk. Knock it off?' You're the doofus, if you think I'm saying that," replied Tony.

"I think we're getting off track, here, Tony. It has to do with good intentions, genuinely trying to help each other, really caring about each other and showing that in how we speak truth to each other. It's about good motives for speaking," said Ivy with an imploring look for Tony to genuinely engage.

"Okay, I get it," he nodded. "So we're friends from now on?"

"Friends," she said.

"So now do we take a knife and slice our wrists and rub our blood together?" asked Tony with an eyebrow raised ridiculously high.

"Don't be such a doofus!" she snorted.

Another leadership meeting was called. Some thought they needed to reconsider going out to find vehicle fuel and some food sources. It would take about a month and a half after planting before they could begin harvesting the earliest crops. They needed grain. And they had heard of a doctor and his family who were needing to be rescued. The Farm really needed a doctor. The discussion continued for some time, each weighing the pros and cons. They asked God to show them what He would have them do. No one wanted to jeopardize the camp by taking unnecessary risks. But some also thought that this seeming interlude was the best time to scout out resources before things heated up again, as they surely would. After praying together, they all agreed they didn't have the resources to get through what they anticipated the rest of the time would be, and they did need a doctor. It was getting close to time for Mary Beth to have her baby, and it would be a high-risk delivery. Also, Mrs. Smith was having episodes with multiple issues. She said that she didn't want to risk everybody else's safety, so don't let that be a factor. But if they could help the doctor's family to safety, relatively speaking, and secure a doctor for the camp at the same time—because who knew when something would happen that would require more than first aid—and also obtain supplies? They finally decided to send someone out. There was a huge discussion about just who that would be. It was finally decided that a married couple would be the least obvious, and the title holders of the van should have the best chances if they would be stopped for a routine inspection. John and Sarah Parker agreed to go. It made sense. The city they needed to go to was their own, they knew people that might be sources, and the doctor reportedly was in hiding there. Tony would stay in the camp with Evan and Ivy Thomas. If the Parkers had an opportunity to get information on Louisa Thomas without taking undue risks, they would. Her parents lived there, and that was the last known place she was planning on being. They would drive through the night to be there before dawn. Sarah was torn about leaving Tony. She had no misgivings about Evan and Ivy. Evan was solid and loved Tony, and the kids had made a huge turnaround. Tony and Ivy had become best pals and hung out together every day. They even decided to minister to the younger kids together and organized activities to keep the younger ones occupied through some long days. *But what if we don't make it back?* Sarah's determination nearly failed. John's head told him they had to do something, and they were the most likely to make it if anyone could, but his heart scrunched up in a tight ball inside his chest as he thought about leaving their only child and taking the risk of never coming back. He could hardly breathe, and the look on Sarah's face nearly swept away his resolve. Sarah willed herself to recommit herself to the plan and her confidence in God's leading. They could not be controlled by fear. They had to trust in God, no matter what. John saw her expression change as he watched her face, and he knew they would do this. And he knew that whatever happened, it would be okay. They were in God's hands and God loved Tony even more than they did, as impossible as that seemed. Tony belonged to his heavenly Father. John wrapped his arms around Sarah, "Father—give us the strength to do what you've called us to do. Give us courage when we lack courage. We place our son into your hands. Put a hedge of protection around him. Help Tony to remain faithful to the end. We praise you, heavenly Father. Please hear our prayer. Amen."

Louisa sat looking out the window of her bedroom. This had been her bedroom all of her growing up years. It was so familiar, yet she felt like a stranger to it. And trapped. This wasn't where she belonged. She should be with her husband and daughter, not here. She had feared suffering and death. She had run from it. And ran straight into the jaws of suffering and death. The irony seemed to mock her. The suffering from the wreck had been over a year now. The pain was debilitating at times still, but was somewhat manageable as she continued to heal. The therapy could be horrific, but she made herself endure it, to work hard through it. If God gave her life, then she would hold onto it with both hands and her teeth, even if her legs couldn't take her across her room on her own yet. She would keep working, even though she knew the likelihood of escaping the Beast's officers and finding Evan and Ivy was essentially impossible, even if she were in shape for a marathon. She looked in the mirror and didn't recognize the image she saw there. *God, why did you save me, just to face death again?*

The confirmation that Evan was right hadn't dawned on her for a long time. Then as they began to wean her from the drugs, she became aware that the world had changed. The Beast was in power. There was a one world government and a cashless society. Anyone who wanted to buy or sell had to take the mark on their hand or forehead. If they didn't, they would be killed or put in the work camps until they died. Killed, just a slower death. No one said much about the death camps, but the stories were shown nightly on the news to remind people what happens to the NCC's. Not everyone had been rounded up yet to take or refuse the mark. *Lord, officers are coming tomorrow to get my answer. I have stalled them off as long as I can. I can't work in the death camps, so, they will haul me off to kill me when I refuse to take the mark. Wouldn't it have been easier to just let me die in the wreck?*

The thought came to her of the trip to her parents' house that day. Her realization as she drove that she was a coward, and that she had abandoned her husband and daughter because of her fear of persecution and death. Then the wild compulsion to turn around and go back. And then that horrific sound. She had no recollection of seeing the truck at all, or experiencing pain in that moment, only that explosion of sound. The pain came later. Suffering and pain, Louisa discovered is unavoidable. She also realized that sometimes we can choose to suffer with purpose. Or, the alternative, we can suffer through what life just dishes out, with no choice or purpose, no higher goal than to be purified with the fire of suffering. Evan understood that. He chose to suffer for a higher cause. To give testimony and witness to the God of the universe that He is good and the rightful object of our worship. That God is love and came to save us from the evil that is now ruling the earth and from an eternal hell for standing with Satan. God Himself suffered and died for us. The Bible called it an honor to suffer for Christ's sake. An honor with an eternal reward. *Father, would you give me the courage to suffer with purpose? To suffer for Your name's sake? To be a witness to that great cloud of witnesses watching from heaven? I praise you, Father. I choose You.*

The next day, Lou's parents showed the officers to her room.

"Well, Mrs. Thomas, you seem to be progressing quite well, considering. Have you heard from your husband yet?"

"No, I haven't."

"It seems quite strange that a man would abandon his wife under such difficult circumstances, don't you think?"

"I don't know what to think, sir. We had a disagreement right before I left to come visit my parents. I have been through a lot since then, and don't remember much."

"Your parents have told us that they have checked regularly since the accident, and your husband, Evan Thomas, and your daughter, Ivy, seemed to have abandoned your home with no forwarding address. Can you tell us where they might be, Mrs. Thomas? Where they may have gone?"

"No, sir. I cannot," replied Louisa.

"Is it true, Mrs. Thomas, that your husband held certain beliefs about the Bible that might cause him to become involved with a cult and become noncompliant to our new world order? To maybe join a secret society?"

"No, sir. He believed what was written in the Bible. The truth that is written in the Bible. And I honestly don't know where he is."

"Mrs. Thomas, it is totally unnecessary to play games with us. Our sources have informed us that your husband was very outspoken about his beliefs. Those beliefs are crimes against the state, law and order. We believe he and others, including John and Sarah Parker and their son, Tony, have joined an illegal group and are in hiding with the purpose of inciting treason. Is that why you argued and left the day of your accident? Your parents say that you didn't agree with your husband's beliefs. They suspect you are reluctant to implicate your husband, but that you are loyal to the government. If that is so, you could prove your loyalty and be a great service to society by helping us find him. We have moved beyond the petty values of opposing religions and warring nationalism. We are moving toward a vision of world peace and equality for all. We all must sacrifice our individual self interest for the common good." Lou remained silent.

"So, are you ready, Louisa Thomas, to demonstrate your loyalty to the new world order and its leader by receiving his mark on your hand or forehead?"

"I am not. I refuse," replied Lou evenly and clearly.

"So you are a traitor, also, Mrs. Thomas. No matter, we have ways to extract the information we need from you. Inject her. I don't know why we wasted all that time and resources in healing you, Mrs. Thomas. It seems your parents don't know you as well as they thought."

"They have fallen under the deluding influence instead of believing what the word of God says," replied Lou. "No matter what you do to me, I will not deny my God, and you won't get any information out of me, because I don't know where they are."

"We shall see," replied the officer.

They injected her with the serum and proceeded to interrogate Louisa. After additional means of torture failed to get the information they were seeking, the under officer said, "I guess she doesn't know where they are. She's answered all the other questions accurately, and even admitted their association with the Parkers, but she doesn't know where they are. I don't think she is strong enough to last another round."

"What a waste. Finish her."

Dr. Goldman, his son-in-law, and his grandson, all sat in the back of the van. Containers of grain and cans of fuel were behind them. John and Sarah sat in front. They did not go to the Johnson's.

Their sources said Louisa had been terminated the day before for refusing the mark. Her parents had publically denounced her. They had one more stop to make to pick up medical supplies that had been arranged at the drug store before heading back to the Farm with the Goldman family. Both John and Sarah had disguised themselves with sunglasses and hats. But Rube Goldman had specific orders to take the wheel and calmly drive away if anything went wrong. They were not to stop until they got the supplies to the Farm.

As they approached the store, John opened the door for Sarah, who was standing off to the side. An older lady from inside, supposing he was holding it for her to come out, hurried through the door, colliding with Sarah with considerable impact, knocking off both her hat and sunglasses. The older woman nearly fell in the scramble, and Sarah reached out to grab her. As they came face to face, Sarah discovered she was looking into the face of Lou's mother, Clara Johnson.

"Why, Sarah Parker!" exclaimed Clara. Sarah watched the expressions flicker across Clara's face—astonishment and then realization. "Help! Somebody help! This woman is a traitor!" Immediately both men and women surrounded her, as John stepped up beside her and slipped his arm around Sarah's waist. As the police began to arrive, to John's relief, he saw his van slowly pull out of its parking place and drive away. And then he saw his brother get out of a squad car and gave orders for the people to step back and ordered the first officers who responded, to cuff Sarah and John and take them to the station.

Chapter FIVE

O n the way to the station, John and Sarah spoke quietly to each other in the back seat. They went over the contingency plans. They decided if they had a chance to make a break, they would. If they got shot, then the suffering would be brief and they wouldn't have a chance of exposing the Farm. If not, then they had to pray that God would help them to not reveal the location of the Farm. Louisa had not known, so she could not have betrayed them under the influence of the drugs. They shared their love for one another and their conviction of seeing each other soon in paradise. They prayed and asked God to give them the strength to be faithful to the end. Then they prayed for their only son, Tony. And as Sarah looked into John's eyes, both had tears welling up and they began to softly sing, "Amazing grace, how sweet the sound that saved a wretch like me. I once was lost, but now I'm found, was blind, but now I see." John reached over and took Sarah's hand and gently raised it to his lips. "Father, please be Father to our son, and as you said in Daniel 11, 'Those who have insight among the people will give understanding to the many; yet they will fall by the sword and by flame, by captivity and by plunder for many days. Now when they fall they will be granted a little help...' we need your help, Father, to not expose the Farm. And give to those remaining an outpouring of your Spirit to bring salvation to those who have not yet taken the mark."

As they arrived at the station, John's younger brother was standing in the parking lot, waiting. He ignored the prisoners and gave instructions to the officer who brought them in. He took them into the station and they were booked and charged with treason, a capital offense. Afterward, they were led to an office. The desk had a name plate with the name, Chief of Police, Greg Parker. They sat while the officer guarded the door until Greg Parker, John's younger brother, entered.

"I'm curious, what made you come back?" asked Greg. Neither his brother nor sister-in-law spoke. "No matter. We were going to find you anyway. We thought Louisa would give you up, but there are others who will stumble, like you just did."

Again, neither of the captives spoke, but John noticed the mark both on Greg's hand and forehead. "It won't do you any good to play games. Let me tell you how this is going to work. You will be placed into an interrogation cell. You will be able to see what is happening to each other and the result on the other for refusing to answer questions. I hope you are both strong in your resolve, because I want to watch you suffer. Like you caused our mother to suffer."

Finally, John spoke. "What do you mean?"

"Mother didn't go with you because she thought she would be a liability, so she stayed, knowing what it meant. She refused the mark. They tortured her, but she didn't know anything, so they shot her in the head, right in front of me. I hated you, John. Hated you for leaving. Hated you for convincing Mother that there is life after death for the faithful followers of Jesus—what a crock. And hated you for causing her suffering. I decided right then and there, that if I ever had a chance to bring this back on you, I would. So when they stood in front of me with the mark, I stuck out my hand and then pointed to my forehead. I would be the best damned agent for the Beast and I was going to find you and make you suffer. So, how about let's get to the suffering part?"

In the interrogation room, John and Sarah were positioned in chairs across the room from one another so the "doctors" had ample room to work on their victims.

"We aren't going to use the serum at first," said Greg. "Not enough suffering. Besides, we've lost too many that way before we extracted the information we wanted. So we will go the slow, old fashioned way. Shall we begin with the toe and fingernails?"

"Father—please—a little help, for both of us," was the silent prayer John sent up as the "doctors" began selecting their tools.

Sometime later, Greg stood up, tiring of the spectacle. Sarah just kept passing out and it was getting hard to bring her back around. That was defeating the leverage they had with John. So he was bearing up and showing no signs of cracking, even though he would scream during the extractions, he would sing or quote scripture between. Oh, well, there was a whole list of techniques he had developed in preparation for this. Maybe move on to the next step.

Evan was in the courtyard when the Parker's van pulled into the compound. Someone else was driving. He ran to the van. Where were the Parkers? Pastor arrived and called some of the leadership together. They went into his office to debrief the three men.

"Evan, we have news of Louisa," said Pastor when they all emerged from his office. Please come in so we can talk in private."

"What happened?" asked Evan.

"Sarah and John were taken at the last stop," he replied. The Goldmans stayed in the van with instructions to pull away and drive here if anything went wrong. They saw an older woman bump into Sarah on her way through the door, knocking Sarah's disguise off. The woman immediately recognized her and began yelling for help that Sarah was a traitor. People surrounded them and police showed up almost as soon as it happened. The youngest Goldman had his cell phone and snapped a picture of the scene as they left. This is the picture. We downloaded his phone before we disabled it."

Evan took it and studied the picture. "That's my mother-in-law, Clara Johnson. Of course she would recognize Sarah. We've been close friends for years. But I am shocked to see John's younger brother, Greg, in a police uniform stepping out of the squad car."

Pastor took the picture and intently studied the picture. "They gathered information on Louisa while they were in town, John. The Goldmans didn't know her, but John and Sarah shared the information they obtained."

"Tell me," said Evan.

"The story they got was that on the day she left and you came here, it was raining and suddenly she attempted to do a U turn in the middle of the highway. The semi driver that hit her said she just came out of nowhere. There was no missing her. She was very seriously mangled and she was not expected to live through the night. But she did, and very slowly she began to recover and started rehab. Her parents took her to their house when she was able to leave the hospital and do outpatient rehab. The authorities had been holding off questioning her and presenting the mark because of her weakened condition, but just two days before Parker's arrived, her death was announced. She had been questioned and refused the mark. One of the officers at the scene had complained to someone associated with our source that waiting for her to recover had produced no information, and that Greg Parker had been furious that she hadn't yielded anything before they exterminated her after she refused the mark. And afterward her parents publically denounced her. I am so sorry to have to give you this news, Evan," offered Pastor.

Evan buried his face in his hands. His shoulders shook violently as his sobs escaped into the room. Pastor came around his desk and put his arms around Evan. Some minutes later, Evan sat in his chair trying to collect himself, pulling out a handkerchief to blow his nose. His chest still heaved when he replayed the words he'd just heard. The emotions hit him in waves as he thought of her changing her mind and turning around, and the collision that robbed them of being reunited. Of her suffering all these months and him not knowing—not being there for her. The guilt, the sorrow. The relief. Then the guilt about feeling relieved. Relieved that she had refused the mark, even though it meant her death. She was alive! She had entered into life and they could spend eternity together, if not as husband and wife, but surely as the deep friends they had grown to become. He had been so afraid that she would take the mark as she had said before she left the house that day. He had prayed and prayed, having no idea how to pray, except that above all else, she would remain faithful to the end. Evan knelt down in front of his chair and worshipped God.

"Ivy," Evan finally spoke. "I need to tell Ivy. I don't know how to even begin. And Tony. Dear God! Both of his parents and no one else in the world to call family! We know his grandma was exterminated by the beast because she refused the mark, and it was clear from the report that his uncle, Greg, had been deceived by the Beast."

"Would you like me to go with you, Evan?" asked Pastor.

"Let me talk with Ivy alone, first," said Evan. "And then maybe you can be with us to talk to Tony. But do we know anything except that they were arrested?"

"That's all at this point," replied Pastor. "We may hear more. It was a very public arrest, and they were wanted by the police, so they may make a case of it to the public. From a human standpoint, it doesn't look good. If they survive the torture, they may send them to the work camps, or they may do a public execution. But we will pray, because all things are possible with God, and He does say that a remnant will be saved alive out of this...'then we who are alive and remain will be caught up together with them in the clouds to meet the Lord in the air, and so we shall always be with the Lord.'"

"Pastor, Louisa couldn't give information because she didn't know where the Farm is. Sarah and John do know, and several other Farms and sources. I really don't think they will break under torture, but if they use the drugs on them, it no longer is a matter of will or loyalty. The drugs just take over."

"Yes, Evan. It is in God's hands. He has a plan and we must trust Him. This is part of the purification process. We all need to pray that we can have the courage to trust Him, even in the darkest hour. That no matter what happens, we will keep faith and be faithful to the end, like your dear Louisa did. We will keep our eyes fixed on Jesus, the author and finisher of our faith, who went ahead of us, and calls us to follow Him. To love and forgive our enemies and pray for them. And that we can lead many more to Christ, even if it costs our lives. Now, you go to Ivy and then let me know when you want me to join you and Tony."

"Will he see the van is back?" asked Evan, wondering if Tony would catch on before they had a chance to talk with him.

"No. It is parked in the shed," replied Pastor. "The Goldmans have been taken to their room until the camp can be informed and too many questions are flying. I will be praying for the children's hearts, Evan, and for your words. Go now, before people begin talking."

Evan held Ivy tightly in his arms as they both wept together. He had withheld some of the details, but had been forthright. She seemed grateful to know that her mom had changed her mind and had tried to come back to them. She also seemed relieved to know that her mom had refused the mark. They talked a little about what their reunion in heaven would be like, taking comfort in that.

Finally, Ivy said, "Dad... I really don't know if I even want to forgive those people, you know, our enemies. The people who killed Mom."

"I do understand that, Ivy. When someone wrongs us or does evil, we feel we have a right--that they deserve our hate or unforgiveness, especially when it is so evil and intentional. I guess that is why God's love so amazes me. He is so pure and good, and yet Satan, in the hearts of evil men killed him; and not accidentally, either. Jesus hung on that cross, having no sin of his own, not deserving any punishment whatsoever. He did it for us. He went to the cross for our sins. Because He wanted to save us. He wanted to save those who killed Him, too, because He understood that they were under Satan's influence and didn't realize that they were his minions, serving Satan without understanding they were killing the Son of God who loved them and came from heaven to save them. So, He said as He hung there, 'Father, forgive them, for they don't know what they're doing.' And that is amazing to me, Ivy."

"But that was Jesus; He is perfect."

"Yes," replied Evan. "But He does teach us to become like Him. That happens one decision at a time. He forgave so we are to forgive. And He says only God knows people's hearts, thoughts, and intentions, so we need to leave judgment to Him— and God will judge everyone, Ivy. Teaching us to forgive doesn't give them a pass. It simply acknowledges that we are forgiven and need to have a forgiving and grateful heart and want forgiveness and eternal life for every other human being. Because from the day we were born, we all were headed for hell if it wasn't for Jesus, and Satan wants to ruin us and drag every one of us into eternal punishment with him. He hates it when we forgive. Do you know why?"

"No...Because he hates us?"

"Well, that is true, Ivy. But what I was asking is, do you understand why Satan hates for us to forgive people who wrong us?"

"No, I don't know that, either," replied Ivy.

"Think about what Jesus teaches at the end of Matthew 18."

"What?"

"Jesus tells a story of a slave who owed his king a whole lot of money. The king decided it was time to settle up his accounts, but this man owed him so much money that he could never pay him back. So he ordered that the slave should be sold, along with his wife and children to get some of the money the slave owed him. The slave went to the king and fell on his face before the king and begged and pleaded with the king to have patience with him and he would repay him everything. Well, the king felt compassion for the man and decided to release him and forgive all his debt. Afterward, that slave went out and found another slave who owed him way less money than he had owed the king, and started choking him and demanded the other slave repay him. The other slave begged for patience and that he would repay him. The first slave said no and had the second slave thrown into prison until he paid him back all he owed him. Well, all the other slaves who saw this and knew that the king had forgiven the first slave were upset and went and told the king. The king was very angry and called the first slave and told him that since the king had forgiven the slave all the debts he owed the king when he pleaded with the king, that the slave should have had mercy on the other slave who owed the first slave money. Then the king handed the slave over to the torturers until he should repay all that was owed him. Then Jesus says, 'My heavenly Father will also do the same to you, if each of you does not forgive his brother from your heart.'"

"Man, that seems harsh, but the slave was a jerk and deserved it, I guess," said Ivy.

"Now think about it, Ivy. What happens to us if we won't forgive others?"

"God won't forgive us."

"Who will that make happy?" asked Evan.

"Satan, I guess," she replied.

"Yes. He is delighted, because he gets two for one. Not only is the sinner doomed, if he doesn't repent, but the one the sinner sinned against is also doomed, because he has taken on the role of Satan. You see, unforgiveness means we judge the other person and want them to be punished. We think we are punishing them with our hate and unforgiveness. We may even do something to them to hurt them. Like spread rumors about them, or try to turn other people against them, or even physically hurt them. But in reality, we are only hurting ourselves. We become bitter, ugly people like Satan, trying to take our own vengeance and forgetting we are sinners also who need forgiveness. In the process, if we hold to our unforgiveness, we also become unforgiven, because God won't give to us what we won't give to others. Jesus coming from heaven to be tortured and hung on a cross so we can be forgiven and to defeat the wickedness of Satan was His whole purpose. If we decide to oppose Christ's work on the cross by not forgiving others, then we are fighting on Satan's side and will fall under God's judgment ourselves. It is serious business, Ivy—standing against God."

"I never thought of it that way," said Ivy. "What if I don't feel like it—forgiving them? I know I should, but what if I don't feel like it?"

"The first step is to agree with God. He says we are all sinners and deserve hell. When I acknowledge that, I have a right perspective about myself. I have done wrong things and I need and want to be forgiven for them. I want Jesus' blood to apply to my sin. I have to make a decision. In reality, I am no different from the person who wronged me. So, if I am fair minded, or just, as the Bible would say, then I have to admit we are both in the same boat and we both need forgiveness—man's and God's. So then I tell God that. And ask Him to help me forgive my enemy from my heart and I need to ask God to forgive them, too. Just like Jesus did on the cross." With tears in his eyes, Evan looked deep into his daughter's eyes. "I need to do that, Ivy. We have some hard things ahead of us and I need to settle this right now in my heart, because thoughts of your mom will come back and it will hurt. But I know we will be together again if I make the right decisions. What about you, Ivy? Will you pray with me before we leave this room? There is a lot going on out there and we will need God's help to be to Tony what he needs. We will be Tony's family now."

Tears fell from Ivy's eyes as she nodded her head.

Chapter SIX

After they found the pastor, the three of them went to find Tony. He wasn't in their room, and no one had seen him. Ivy suggested they look at the pond. Tony was sitting on the bench picking weeds apart and tossing them on the ground. When they walked up, Tony looked up and it was evident that he had been crying.

"Tony," Evan began.

"I already know," interrupted Tony. "Don't say it."

"How?" asked Ivy.

"I came to our room and heard you and your dad talking. About your mom. So I figured they must have got back from the trip and went looking for Mom and Dad. I found the van in the shed and then I saw the three new men being taken to a room. Mom and Dad didn't come back, did they?" asked Tony.

"No, son. They got discovered on their last stop and were taken and arrested. The Goldmans followed the instructions your parents had given them, and drove away," said Pastor.

Tony heaved the remaining weeds at the pond and slumped off the bench to the ground. "Why? Why didn't God protect them?" he wailed. "We're trying to obey Him. Why is He letting Satan pick us off? Doesn't He care? I thought He was supposed to love us and protect us—all that love stuff—hmpf! And if He is supposed to be all powerful, He can stop Satan, can't He, if He wanted to? What's the deal, anyway?"

"Those are all legitimate questions, Tony," answered Pastor. "And it will take a while to answer them, but I think the most important thing is to ask you what is uppermost in your mind right now? What do you want to deal with first? Do you just want some time to absorb this? Do you have questions about this we can talk about?"

As Pastor spoke, Ivy walked over and sat on the ground beside Tony. She took his hand in hers, and they both hugged each other and wept. Through her tears and sobs, Ivy managed to say, "You are my little brother now, Tony. We will be family. We kind of were anyway, but now it's real. Got that? We belong to each other."

Evan sat on the other side of Tony and put his arm around his shoulder. "I know I can never take your parents' place, Tony. But I would be honored to be a dad to you and to love you like the son I never had. I know that's a bit much to take in right now, but I just want you to know that as you process what has happened. You are not alone. You have people, a family—if you will have us." Tony studied the grass between his feet as he listened, feeling like he was in some other dimension, some weird altered state that inside he knew couldn't be true, but also knew in another part of his mind that, yes, this really was true, and his mind felt too numb to think, let alone respond.

Tony decided to not attend the meeting where the new members would be introduced. He just needed to be alone for a while. Not have to talk, or answer questions, or endure the sympathetic looks of the other residents. He just felt too numb to deal with the overwhelming emotions and thoughts that weighed on his mind. He just wanted to crawl into his bed, pull the blanket over his head, go to sleep and never wake up. And later he would scream and tear a tree apart limb from limb and throw them like javelins into the heavens at the God who allowed this to happen.

Although Evan and Ivy really didn't feel like socializing, when Tony wanted to be alone, they decided to go to the meeting. The meeting had already begun when they arrived. The three new-comers were being introduced as Evan and Ivy sat down in the back row: Dr. Abrahim Goldman, his son-in-law, Rube Lehman, a Christian rabbi and expert in Old Testament writings, and (thought Ivy), a very handsome (her friends would say "hot") grandson, named Jacob. Dr. Goldman explained that his wife had contracted a rare genetic disease that led him into genetic research to find a cure for his wife. In the process, the government had solicited his help with some of their projects on global pandemics and genetic alterations, promising him support and funding for his research if he helped them. He agreed, but in the meantime, his wife succumbed to the disease. The government's projects overtook the Doctor's research, and he found his time consumed with them. When the Corona research came under scrutiny for ethics issues from Congressional oversight commit-tees, the research was moved to China under the oversight of the WHO and the National Institutes of Health and was funded indirectly by some of the wealthiest people in the world whose agenda was to create a pandemic that would create a need for a vaccine from which they hoped to profit greatly. Dr. Goldman became aware that they intended to use the vaccine as a carrier for sterilization drugs for global population control as well, and that they intended to make the vaccine mandatory for everyone in the world. The rationale was to "protect" the world from the virus, monitor and limit travel, quarantine segments and individuals of the population, and create a data bank of personal information and requirement of a chip inserted into every person on the planet that contained their personal data and ability to track their whereabouts.

"I refused to work on this research," said Dr. Goldman. "They couldn't force me, since I had the oversight committee decision in my favor, so they proposed a different genetic research project that I had previously been unfamiliar with. It was a collaboration between U.S. military and private industry. This research focused on genetic engineering on many organisms, but what they wanted help with was genetically enhancing humans—particularly as soldiers. Other countries were in this race for the invincible, self-healing soldier as well. I opted out when I found out what they were doing. Since then, threats were made. Financial pressure came to bear. My appointment to other research has been blackballed. False accusations about my finances have been made by the IRS, and my bank accounts have been frozen and funds removed. When I had continued to refuse this research project, my daughter met an untimely death that was not an accident. They ruled it a suicide, but that absolutely was not the case. She was murdered because I refused to cooperate." It seemed to be very difficult for this elderly gentleman to relate his story, and his voice broke. His son-in-law rose from his chair with tears welling up in his eyes to continue the story. They had gone into hiding, grandfather, son-in-law and grandson until they could decide what to do. Through his connections with an element of the Christian church that was anticipating the end times as prophesied in scripture, believing the re-establishment of Israel as a nation and Jerusalem returning to Israel as its capital, signified the end was most likely near, he was told of a system of "Farms" of refuge for believers. The "Farms" were in the process of being established, and due to the imminent danger to their lives, the Goldmans were established at a Farm during its initial set up. They had been there until the Farm got word that the authorities were preparing to raid it. In order to keep Dr. Goldman's knowledge out of the hands of the government and the other governments seeking him, they were the first to be sent out. Others got out also, but many soon afterward were captured and imprisoned or killed. The Goldmans had a rendezvous with the Parkers that went off smoothly until their last stop before returning to the farm. Because the Parkers had given them specific directions if anything went wrong at the last stop and they were apprehended, they were to drive away as inconspicuously as possible. They were not to try to intervene and risk their own capture and lose the supplies for the Farm they were carrying.

"We extend our greatest sympathy for your loss of John and Sarah Parker. They risked their lives for us. They were strong and courageous, and they were the image of Christ to us. Please accept our heartfelt gratitude for accepting us into your circle," finished Rube. The grandson, Jacob, did not speak during the meeting.

The people mingled afterward and clustered in small groups quietly discussing this news. Ivy and Evan moved toward the front. The news of Louisa had also been announced, and many offered their condolences. It seemed awkward to both Evan and Ivy. They simply nodded their heads and said thank you. When they reached the Goldmans, they introduced themselves. The two young people were trying to assess each other without being too obvious. Ivy smiled, and Jacob, somewhat stiffly, nodded. Ivy volunteered to show Jacob around the farm, so he followed her out the door. When they reached the pond, they sat on the bench that had been occupied very recently by Tony. She wondered how Tony was doing.

"So your mom was Louisa?" asked Jacob.

"Yes."

"I'm very sorry, Ivy," replied Jacob. "She must have been very brave. I don't know if I could have remained strong like she did."

Ivy involuntarily caught her breath. Jacob quickly apologized, stumbling over his words of regret for being insensitive to her new loss. "Well, today just confirmed our fears," replied Ivy. "It's a long story, but Mom didn't come with us, and we haven't known what had happened to her all this time. It was such a blow to hear it today, but it was also a relief in a way, to have an answer to the agonizing questions that just kept spinning in my head. Logic said she couldn't have survived all that time unless she took the mark, but no word came about her. I hate it that she had to suffer alone, but I am so glad she didn't take the mark. Now I know I will see her again soon." Ivy paused before she spoke, "And it was so good to hear she had tried to turn around and come back to us before the wreck," choked Ivy as she fought the tears and lost. Jacob put a tentative hand on her shoulder and then quickly removed it. What could he say that wouldn't sound plain stupid? So he stayed silent.

"I'm sorry," said Ivy. "This must be awkward for you—me blubbering in front of you."

"I just know that words can sound so hollow. The pain and sorrow are so enormous. Even the truth and promises of God can seem empty during the first shock. At least that's how I felt when my mom was killed."

"Here I am, just thinking of myself when you lost your mom, too. And Tony—he just found out both of his parents were taken. You haven't met him yet. He wanted to be alone after he got the news."

"I haven't met him, but John and Sarah spoke of him. They seemed so proud of him. They seemed to have a great love for each other and their love for Tony was just so real—like a natural extension of their love for each other, but with a unique treasuring of their son."

"He probably needs to hear that," said Ivy. "He's having lots of questions about God's love, and he may begin asking himself why they took this mission and left him. It is easy in the pain to become angry at whoever and whatever. I know I was after we got here. I didn't know what to do with this whole thing—not knowing about Mom, wondering how she could have left us, mad at her, and yet feeling guilty about being mad, and missing her so much; the ache and emptiness just wouldn't go away. So I took it out on Tony. I was really a schmuck. My friends at school would have a different name for it. I was a real jerk."

"Let's go find him and just sit with him," suggested Jacob.

They found Tony lying on his bed, staring at the ceiling, absently running his fingers through Leroy's fur, whose head was propped on the middle of Tony's chest.

"Tony, this is Jacob Lehman," said Ivy. "He's new here. He wanted to meet you."

Tony shrugged his shoulders and kept staring at the ceiling. "Why?"

"I wanted to tell you what fine people your parents are," said Jacob. "I owe my life to them."

"Were. My parents were. And I don't like the trade. Okay?" replied Tony.

"Sure. I get it," answered Jacob.

"Tony, we'll give you more time," said Ivy. "When you feel like talking, we'll be around. We have all lost parents, Tony. And we are all on the same side. We need to remember that."

Leroy lifted his head and watched them leave the room.

Chapter SEVEN

Tony either stayed in his bed or down by the pond for the next three days without a word to anyone except a grunt when necessary. Ivy invited Jacob to join her with the activities that she and Tony had developed for the children. They talked about their "old" lives and friends and activities before everything changed. It became clear to Jacob that Ivy had struggled to fit in and make friends due to her religious upbringing and the tighter supervision that her parents had maintained that kept her from doing a lot of things most of her classmates did. Because Jacob was an athlete, and he was willing to push the bounds of his parents' rules and the truth, his school experience was very different from Ivy's. He knew he was attractive. He had a good build, he was better than average in school, and if he turned his attention to a girl, he was confident that she would date him. Ivy had never dated and he could see that look in her eyes when she looked at him. And it troubled him. Not that Ivy was unattractive to him. She wasn't a knockout, but a guy could do a lot worse if he was looking. *But you're not looking, remember, Studly? Yeah, I'm talking to you, Studly. Hard to quit, isn't it? You've caused quite enough trouble for the rest of your life, however long that may be, so just don't go there. She's a good kid, so you just keep it that way, okay,*

Studly? Jacob shook his head to himself and turned his attention back to the three-legged race he was supervising.

"How's it going?" asked Ivy as she approached Jacob with her troupe of little girls following like a bunch of gaggling goslings. *Where did I come up with that, Jacob wondered. Only 4 days in and I'm flaking off.*

"This finishes the last race," replied Jacob. "What now?"

"Time for the kids to go back to the classroom to finish their morning studies," she said. Ivy headed toward the pond. It was the place of refuge away from the activity of the camp, a place where one could reflect alone, or have a quiet conversation, or read a book without all the comings and goings that are required to keep a community of people living. Jacob automatically followed along. She sat on the bench, and after his recent conversation with himself, he sat on the ground with his back against a large oak tree. As if on cue, Ivy asked, "Jacob, have you ever had a real girl friend?"

Here it comes, Studly. Where are you going to take this? "Yes, I have, Ivy."

"I think that is one of the big things I regret. I had really hoped that I would fall in love and get married and have kids—you know—just everyday normal life. I was expecting to have a life. Don't get me wrong, heaven sounds great, and I do love God, but it makes me so sad that I am going to miss my life. Do you ever think about that? You know, the no marriage in heaven thing?"

"Actually, Ivy, I have. A lot," replied Jacob.

"So, like what? What do you think about it?"

"At first I felt cheated. I really wasn't a dedicated Jewish Christian like my family. In fact, if I was honest, I tried to avoid it as much as possible. Kept involved in sports and parties and drinking. I didn't do much drugs, but some, but was careful so I wouldn't get in trouble or kicked out of sports. My friends and I all watched pornography. I didn't bring any attention to my family's religion, and if anyone decided to make it an issue, I knew how to shut them up—make them look like an idiot, pick out some flaw to turn the attention back on them and ridicule them. Totally diverted the attention. As far as the girls, I never had any trouble getting dates. For me, it was about sex. Didn't treat them right, and when I got bored, got somebody else." Jacob was speaking more to the pond than to Ivy, but her stricken look was not lost on him as he continued.

"Then I found a girl I kind of liked. Her name was Amy. We dated regularly for almost a year. I could have sex whenever I wanted it and didn't have to go through all the dating-some-body-new hassles. When I was a senior, she told me she was pregnant. I was furious! And scared. I saw my future dissolve in front of me. I thought of my religious family and how this would affect them and their ministry. I decided this simply couldn't happen. Amy begged me to marry her and raise the baby together. I refused and pushed her away. Told her I'd never see her again if she didn't get rid of it. Told her I wouldn't claim it and say she slept with other guys, too, and she had, too, when we had a fight and broke up once. We both had, just to hurt each other. I watched her wither under my bullying and threats. She got help from the school counselor to go to another town for the abortion. I found out later she died in a motel room alone after they botched the abortion. She was so ashamed, she decided to tell her parents she was staying with a friend and just got a motel room without asking anyone to go with her."

Ivy sat absolutely still, staring at the pond. Finally, "How awful," escaped her lips.

"I am sure you hate me now, Ivy, and rightly so. I hate myself. But it made me think a lot about my behavior, and the act of sex, and sex in our culture. I started reading what the Bible has to say about it, and I have to say I have a completely different viewpoint than I used to."

Ivy's mouth and throat had gone dry, and she croaked out the words, "In what way?"

"I've come to understand that what we practice as sex and love is pretty much the opposite of what God intended. It is fallen just like everything else. I think God can redeem it also, but it is pretty much practiced for selfish reasons, not what I would call 'love' in the manner God would have us love one another. Even the best of circumstances, it seems to me, are driven by motives like satisfying the flesh, feeling wanted and loved, filling whatever needs in us that can be filled by sex, or for girls, a relationship that gives them a sense of worth and value and dulls the sense of loneliness in us—just someone to do things with, even if we have to trade our bodies for it. I don't think that is what God intended in the beginning. I think if a couple is intentional about being transformed in that area of their lives and invite God into it, that it maybe can approximate what God intended, but I don't see much evidence of that."

Some spit had returned to Ivy's mouth, so she decided to try to speak again. "I don't understand what you mean, Jacob," was all she got out.

"The Bible says that sex is to be practiced within the bounds of marriage. So that is rule number one. That protects the family and provides a permanent nurturing environment for the children that sex produces. The family is supposed to be the center for training children to be decent human beings and citizens and to know God. Marriage is the place where two people are to become one in fidelity. It trains us to be faithful to our word, to relationship, to give yourself in trust to another human being in a way that we don't to any other person on the planet. To be partners on the same team, protecting and caring for each other, and supporting each other. It is the relationship that is supposed to lift each other up to God for growth, for healing, and for forgiveness. It is the relationship where we should honor and cherish each other, not use each other. But that is only from the human side," finished Jacob. He looked a little self-conscious about going off on a soap box.

"That's a lot," said Ivy. "It makes sense, but what do you mean, 'the human side'?"

"I'm not sure I understand it all, but there is a spiritual side, and I'm not sure I can explain it so it comes out right, you know, without sounding kinky."

"Kinky?" parroted Ivy.

"You know, twisted, perverted." answered Jacob.

"What do you mean?" asked Ivy.

Jacob took a deep breath and held it. As he let it out, he looked at Ivy to make sure she was paying attention. "Okay. You know how sometimes you hear a preacher talk about the church being the bride of Christ, and talks about the marriage supper of the Lamb?"

"Yes," she said slowly, as she nodded her head just as slowly— as if to say, aaand…

"Are you telling me you've never thought about that? That it's kind of weird?"

"Not really, I guess I've just never really given it any thought at all," she replied.

"Well maybe it's a guy thing. It always kind of creeped me out thinking about being Jesus' bride."

Ivy looked at Jacob with a furrowed brow. "You said it's spiritual. Let's get back to the spiritual side you were talking about."

"Exactly. Well in the book of Ephesians, chapter 5, Paul talks about the marriage relationship and he tells husbands to love their wives like Jesus loves the church. And then at the end of the chapter he says about marriage that the two shall become one flesh, so of course I'm thinking sex. But in the next verse, Paul says that it's a great mystery, but that he is speaking about Christ and the church. Well, that kind of threw me. So I'm thinking about that. But what I know—or think I know from I Corinthians chapter 15—about heaven is that our resurrected bodies will be sown in the flesh, a natural body, but will be resurrected a spiritual body that is imperishable. And we know there won't be sex in heaven—or marriage, as it says. So I'm thinking about all this, and I decided Paul must be talking about a spiritual union with Jesus—the mystery he speaks of—becoming one with Jesus. Then I found Jesus' prayer in John chapter 17 where Jesus prays this whole big prayer about us becoming one with Him and the Father. And I suddenly realized that God gave us marriage and sex to get an idea of the close, driven desire to be with and spend time with Him. To experience Him. To be thrilled with Him as He is with us—to KNOW Him. Marriage and sex are a type of what we can have with Him. And will have with Him in heaven. And with the others who are there with us. And there it won't be selfish and twisted and perverted. It will be pure, not driven by the flesh, but filled with intimacy, and joy and exhilaration, and love. No, Ivy. I no longer feel cheated at all. I don't think we will miss a thing. Our flesh won't be driven by sex. We will love out of pure motives untainted by the fall. We will be thrilled and satisfied beyond belief. We will have an eternal family of kind and faithful people who will never use us, or abuse us, or fail us or hurt us in any way. We will have the peace of knowing we are loved and belong and the security that we no longer have to strive for acceptance. We are treasured."

Tears streamed down Ivy's cheeks. "Thank you, Jacob."

Chapter EIGHT

"So—where's your hunk, Miss Ivy?" asked a snarky Tony. "I think I liked silence better," replied Ivy.

"I can arrange that," said Tony.

"Oh, Tony, don't be this way. I don't want to fight. I want you back," pleaded Ivy. "Please can't we just talk? I've missed you."

"Yeah, sure. I noticed. You didn't waste any time replacing me with your new hunk. Now you don't need me. You got a replacement for the kids' activities, someone to take long walks with and hang out with. Don't tell me you missed me," snarled Tony.

"Oh, for crying out loud! Don't be stupid! You are my brother. And I don't have a hunk, anyway. If you are talking about Jacob, he is a friend, and I'm grateful for him. He would like to be your friend, too, if you'd let him. We all need each other, Tony, or did you forget who the enemy is?"

"I haven't figured that out yet, Ivy. Or did you forget that almighty, all knowing God somehow let my parents and your mom just slip through the cracks!"

Ivy just stood and looked at Tony. "I understand you are angry, Tony. But you might think about where your anger should be rightfully directed. God didn't kill our parents. Satan did that. He used your uncle and he has deceived most of the whole pathetic, crazy world. But even they are not the enemy, Tony, and you know that. Don't let Satan twist you up, too. Don't take his side just like Adam and Eve did from the beginning. Somehow Satan always tries to make God the bad guy, when it is Satan who is our enemy. Satan is the one who stole our souls and put us in slavery to him. Jesus is the one who came and bled and died to buy us back to deliver us from an eternity in hell. Satan is the one who wraps his chains tighter and tighter to keep us in his clutches—to drag us into hell with him. No, Tony. Don't you blame God. He is our only hope. He is working this out. He has already proven Himself. It is our part to be patient and trust Him till it's finished. This isn't all there is. We are just passing through here until we get home. Don't lose sight of that fact, Tony. You will be with your parents again. They are waiting for you. And so is Mom."

Tony jerked like he'd just been slapped. His eyes pierced through Ivy. He threw the door open and left without a word.

Tony headed toward the pond, with Leroy right beside him. There were a couple of moms and their kids at the bench, so Tony headed for the timber side of the pond. He needed undistracted time to think. He sat on a fallen log and began to think. *Okay, God, maybe you are not the cause of my parents' death, but you could have stopped it. I believe that. So that must mean that I do believe in you. But if you love me, and you are who you say you are, why did you leave me alone?*

"I didn't. I will never leave you or forsake you."

Tony looked around. Nobody there. *I didn't say that out loud and if I heard what I think I heard, I heard it, but it wasn't out loud. Was that you God, or am I losing my marbles?* Silence. Tony waited. *Maybe I just imagined it. I'm an idiot.*

"I have loved you with an everlasting love, Tony. You are the apple of my eye. You are my son. I have called you by name."

Tony forgot to care if anyone was close enough to hear. "If you love me, why are you punishing me like this?"

"My son, do not regard lightly the discipline of the Lord, nor faint when you are reproved by Him; for those whom the Lord loves He disciplines, and He scourges every son whom He receives."

"But why?" Tony cried out. "What did I do?"

"It is for discipline that you endure; God deals with you as with sons; for what son is there whom his father does not discipline? But if you are without discipline, of which all have become partakers, then you are illegitimate children and not sons."

"But this is too hard!"

"You have not yet resisted to the point of shedding blood in your striving against sin."

"Well Mom and Dad did, didn't they?" shot back Tony.

"Yes."

Tony's breath caught and he fell to his knees. Tony sobbed and sobbed until he was spent in a crumpled heap on the ground. He really had no idea how much time had passed, but finally he got back up on his knees and looked up. "God are you still here?"

"I told you, I will never leave you or forsake you. I am always here. I am with you always, Tony, even to the end of the age, when things will get really bad. He who endures to the end will be saved."

"But how can I? I'm not strong enough!"

"Like your parents did. Fix your eyes on Jesus, the author and perfecter of faith, who for the joy set before Him endured the cross, despising the shame, and has sat down at the right hand of the throne of God. He did that for you, Tony, and He asks you to follow Him and become a fisher of men."

"It seems so hard, I don't know if I can do it."

"All discipline for the moment seems not to be joyful, but sorrowful; yet to those who have been trained by it, afterwards it yields the peaceful fruit of righteousness. And Tony, remember, if you need help, all you have to do is ask, I am right here, living inside of you."

"Didn't Mom and Dad ask? You didn't help them."

"Yes, they did ask. And yes, I did help them. They didn't betray the Farm, Tony. That is what they asked for. And they asked to be faithful witnesses to your uncle—to the very end. He saw them give their lives for the truth of the gospel so others could be saved. And he heard them forgive him for what he had done to them. You need to forgive him, also, Tony. Satan had convinced him that no one would be faithful to Me at the cost of their lives. Just like he had accused Job so long ago. I had to let him test Job so Job could vindicate himself before the great cloud of witnesses of the heavenly trial that has been taking place. Your parents vindicated themselves by their faithful lives with Christ as their mediator, and you will also get that chance, Tony. Cling to me, Tony. I am your salvation, your eternal life. I love you and want you here with Me. Ivy was right. Life on earth is temporary. Do not forfeit your eternal life for a brief time here and eternal suffering in hell. Jesus did the work. Remain faithful to the end and you shall be saved."

Tony heard someone coming through the timber. When he looked up he saw Jacob with a gun over his shoulder carrying a couple of rabbits. Jacob hesitated, not knowing if he was welcome. His last encounter with Tony had not been particularly pleasant.

"Am I intruding?" asked Jacob.

"No, it's fine," replied Tony. "Hey, I know I've been acting like a jerk. I'm sorry."

"I've been hoping we could be friends," said Jacob. "We need all the friends we can get, it seems to me."

"Sure. I've been the only guy my age—well, you are quite a bit older, but at least we can do some of the same stuff. Ivy's been pretty good about shooting baskets and stuff with me, but she's still a girl," laughed Tony.

"Do you hunt?" asked Jacob. "We could go out together if you like. The cooks seem to appreciate some fresh meat. It isn't much for the whole camp, but it's a little protein and gives some meat flavor to the dishes," he said, holding up the two rabbits.

"I've never done it before," replied Tony. "Would you teach me?"

"Not enough ammo to target practice," said Jacob, "but you can go along and see what it's like. Besides, I have been wanting to learn how to set snares and we could do that together. Been thinking if people are snooping around, that might draw less attention than gunfire."

"That makes sense—you know I might have some things that we could use in setting up the snares, too," said Tony, as he cupped his chin in his hand "Things I have picked up and saved in a box under my bed. Let's go take a look."

"I need to clean these rabbits and get them to the kitchen first. I'll just do it out here and keep the mess out of the camp to not draw flies," responded Jacob. "You can watch the first one, then I'll have you do the second one."

Kneeling not far from where Tony had been kneeling before God not too long before, the boys bent to the task with their full attention.

Chapter **NINE**

Jacob was alone today. Tony had stayed in the camp to help Evan with a project. Jacob normally liked having Tony's company, but they were really needing meat, and the quieter, the better. He brought the gun along, just in case he couldn't secure it with quieter methods. The camp had been getting reports of more government activity in the area. He wouldn't use the gun unless he had to. He checked some of their snares and the traps they had made. All were empty. And he hadn't seen any sign of wildlife, so he ventured further than he ever had before. The Farm had a nice timber of its own, but it backed up to a huge state forest. Then Jacob found some deer tracks and a trail they used frequently. He decided to follow it. It was early afternoon, so the deer probably wouldn't be moving much. Probably bedded down or browsing close to where they were bedding down. He stepped carefully, moving into the wind, so he had hope that they wouldn't catch his scent before he could bring one down. What a blessing that would be for the camp. "God, please…"

Jacob heard a twig snap. He stopped and very slowly he turned his gaze in the direction of the sound. His eyes caught sight of a man a short distance away behind some brush. The man stood upright and fixed Jacob in his gaze. Jacob did not recognize the uniform he wore, but it clearly was a uniform of some sort. *Local law enforcement? DNR?* He didn't wonder for long. His mind quickly played his pre-rehearsed story as the man moved toward him. He wondered if he should break and run, but he had immediately seen the gun in his holster. Besides, that would trigger a hunt, and forces would be all over the place and certain exposure of the Farm. If he could just pull off his story.

"What's your name, son?" asked the officer.

"Jace, sir."

"What you doing out here with that gun?"

"Well, my grandpa hasn't been doing well, and was hungry for some meat, so I thought I would look for some game."

"Who's your grandpa, boy?"

"Luke Palmer, sir—lives over yonder on the east side of the forest."

"You are a long way from the Palmer place."

"Yes sir. Haven't seen a thing till I came across these deer tracks. Guess I wandered pretty far from home. Seems like the forest has been pretty well hunted out of small game."

By this time, the officer was less than an arm's reach from Jacob. Jacob sensed he was in jeopardy of being handcuffed and taken into custody. In an instant he knew he couldn't let that happen. For starters, they would find out he wasn't who he said he was. And then the interrogations would begin. If he ran, he would need to run in the opposite direction of the Farm. Better to get shot than captured. This man was heavy, but not fit. Jacob made a quick move, knocking the man back while bringing his own leg behind the man's calves, dumping the officer flat on his back. Jacob took off on a dead run, expecting to hear the gun shot and for a fleeting second wondered what being hit by the bullet would feel like. Instead, he heard the officer talking on his radio giving directions to cut him off in the direction Jacob was running. He dove into a creek gully and followed it some distance until he could make a big circle and cut around behind the officer, away from the Farm. Where he would go from there, Jacob had no idea. But he was on his own. "God help me. Be my hiding place. I need a cleft in the rock." And right in front of him, there it was.

"Has Jacob gotten back yet?" asked Evan. "I was hoping he could help me."

"Haven't seen him," replied Ivy. "What do you need?"

"Well, I finished the shelves in the pantry and wanted to bring a bunch of jars out of the root cellar to save trips for the cooks."

"I can help with that," offered Ivy. "But it's almost dark and Jacob is never gone this long."

Evan, Tony, and Ivy walked together to the root cellar on the far edge of the compound. Evan pushed the wheelbarrow to carry the jars back. Leroy trotted along beside them. Evan parked the wheelbarrow at the top of the steep steps that descended into the deep cave so they could carry the jars up to it. Leroy followed them down the steps, and began whining. As Tony was telling him to go back up and stay out of the way, they heard it. Dirt sifted down from above them. It was a deafening blast. Then another and another. The trio grabbed onto each other, unable to hear each other's cries above the blasts. Evan wrapped his arms around the children and held them tightly. And then it was quiet. Drones. Evan had the kids stay in the cellar as he climbed the steps.

Complete devastation awaited him at the top. The sight was more shocking than the blasts. Bodies and body parts were scattered everywhere. All the buildings were leveled. No sign of life anywhere. Eerie quiet. Until he heard the big trucks rumbling toward the camp. Evan quickly retraced his steps into the recesses of the cave. Tony and Ivy started pelting Evan with questions and Tony started up the steps when the answers weren't coming quickly enough. Evan grabbed his arm and pulled him back. He quickly explained the devastation and that it didn't appear anyone but them had lived through the drone attack. He wanted them to stay in the cellar and stay quiet. He told them troops were coming and they reviewed their plans in case this happened. They could hear voices yelling commands. Evan once again gathered the children in his arms and he prayed for the mercy of God. He prayed that they would be faithful to the end and thanked Jesus for His salvation. He asked that God would help them keep their eyes fixed on Him and to put courage in the place of fear. Peace in their hearts. And finally, he asked God to forgive these people as Christ had forgiven them. They heard tramping steps approaching the cave entrance. Then a soldier stood at the top and lifted his gun. At that moment, Leroy sprung to the top and tackled the soldier just as he released his firepower, cutting Leroy down, falling on top of the soldier. As the soldier struggled to get the mangled dog off of him and get up, Evan quickly topped the steps with his hands up. He thought the soldier was going to shoot him, and as he spoke, the soldier didn't seem to understand him. Another soldier approached. They spoke to each other in another language.

The second soldier turned to Evan and addressed him in English, "Your name!"

Evan told him. The man smiled. "So we have finally found you and your fellow UCC's. It was inevitable, you know. How foolish to hide out like a bunch of children hiding in a closet from their father when they have broken the rules. Come now. Are you alone?"

Evan didn't move. The soldier knocked him aside with the butt of his gun. Tony and Ivy stepped forward and climbed the steps. After a brief search of the cave to make sure there was no one else, they herded the trio back toward what had been the center of the camp where the trucks were parked. There were no others from the camp. Then someone stepped out of a truck and walked toward them. Greg Parker. Tony looked at his uncle and remembered what God had said about forgiving this man who had tortured and killed his own brother and sister-in-law, Tony's Mom and Dad. And Tony decided Satan was not going to get two for one. At least not where Tony was concerned. This pathetic man was not worth Tony's hatred, and sure not worth Tony's own salvation. *What kind of twisted heart would kill his own brother? Someone you shared a bedroom with, played football in the yard and shot hoops in the driveway?*

"*A heart, Tony, that had sin crouching at the door, a heart that yielded to the sin, and it consumed him. Guard your heart, Tony.*"

Then Tony remembered an old movie he saw once. A story about a land under cruel tyranny. The character had been selected to compete in battles for his life. To kill or be killed. He had no choice. He had to participate. He decided he would stay alive as long as he could, and would defend his life, but he would not become a hunter. He would not become like them. He would not let them change him into something he did not want to be, even if it meant he would die. Better to lose his life and gain his soul, than to keep his life and lose his soul. Tony returned his uncle's gaze and forgave him from his heart and prayed for him.

Greg Parker did not speak to his nephew, or Evan or Ivy. He simply stared at them with a penetrating steel hard gaze. He gave orders for them to be incarcerated at a nearby labor camp for re-education. He commented to the officer in their hearing that he did not expect any of them to succeed, though, and take the mark. "They will die as non-compliant criminals."

Chapter TEN

Jacob squeezed himself through the cleft in the rock. He didn't have any idea what was in here. Snakes, a bear, a cougar, a drop-off? But he did know what was behind him. Guns and torture. He had no source of light with him, and it was total blackness in front of him. He was out of sight now, so he decided to just stand still to see if his eyes adjusted to give him any sight at all. He heard a helicopter fly over. He got in here just in time. *Thank you, Father. I feel like David running from Saul.* Slowly his eyes began to adjust. The sliver of light through the cleft from outside cast a bit of light into the interior. He could see there was no pit directly in front of him. He moved slightly sideways and more light entered from the outside. He could see a bit to his left and right. So he stepped aside to let in as much light as possible. It seemed to be a cavern, a good sized room. There were some objects in it, but he couldn't make out what they were. They seemed stationary, so he didn't think there was a threat. As he moved forward, he thought he saw what appeared to be a darker passageway. But there was light coming from the end of it. *Perhaps another exit?* He decided to follow it. Slowly—very slowly. He stubbed his toe on a rock. The noise of it startled him and he gave out a little yell. He stopped. The light disappeared. *Okay, that's not another entrance. There's somebody else in here. With a light. If I continue, he can hear me coming and jump me. Especially since he knows this place and I don't. Why would somebody be in here? A homeless person? A criminal in hiding? I guess I am a criminal in hiding. Maybe he's not a bad person, maybe he's someone like me, just trying to outrun the Beast. That's a big gamble, Jacob, to bet on the goodness of man. What's the alternative? Sit down here and die in the dark? God, I sure wish you would show me what to do.* Jacob waited for quite some time, although he had no idea how long. He knew waiting a few minutes can seem like an eternity. Then he saw the light again and heard a rustling. He stood very still. His heart was pounding, and it made it very difficult to keep his breathing quiet. He saw some dark figures emerge into the passageway. It was difficult to calculate the size of the figures, although they varied in size, he could tell that. He decided they were coming to find him, so he might as well take his chances.

"Hello!" he called. He tried to speak loudly enough to be heard, but not so loud to startle them. But startle them he did. And then he realized they were children, as they scrambled over each other to duck back into wherever it was they came from. The young voices he heard were children's voices. And shushing to each other. The tension drained out of Jacob's muscles. Scared children.

"Hello!" he called again. "My name is Jacob. I won't hurt you. I will stay right here if you will come out and talk to me." Then he had a thought. "I needed a place to hide and God showed me this cleft in the rock. May I hide with you? Maybe we can help each other." It was quiet for a few seconds, then whispers, then louder, more urgent whispers, like a disagreement.

"Look. I can leave if you want me to, but I could really use some help," said Jacob. He figured if he could hear them whispering, they could hear him talk in a low normal voice. The acoustics must be great in here. Something to remember.

Finally the light reappeared with one figure accompanying it. As the figure approached, Jacob could tell it was a teenage boy carrying a knife. He estimated the boy was maybe two or three years younger than himself. Jacob also had a knife, but he had no desire to use it in here. He also had the rifle and a few shells. He left it propped against the wall. He didn't want the boy to feel intimidated or like he had to go on the offensive and be proactive with his knife.

"Hello," Jacob repeated again. "My name is Jacob."

"What you hidin' from?" asked the youth.

"Well," replied Jacob, "I have been living in a camp a little way from here. We are not for the new government, and are trying to avoid coming under their authority. We won't take the mark so we can't buy or sell. So we are trying to make it on our own. I was out hunting today and got caught out away from the camp. The government is looking for me. Maybe you just heard the helicopter go over. I couldn't go back home for fear I would lead them to the camp and put everyone in danger."

"So you led them to us?"

"I didn't know you were here. I just prayed to God to show me a hiding place, and I saw this split in the rock and dived in," replied Jacob. "Why are you here?"

"Same reason as you," said the boy.

"You got a name?" asked Jacob.

"Yeah," But the boy didn't offer it.

"How many are you? Where are your parents?" asked Jacob.

"Y'all askin' a lot a questions," replied the boy.

"Sorry. Do you have anything you want to ask me?"

"Naw. I know who you are. I've seen you huntin'. And we've seen your camp," responded the young man.

"Well then, it would sure be nice to know who you are," pressed Jacob.

The youth gazed steadily at Jacob. "Robert E. Lee, but they just call me Bobby."

"Glad to meet you, Bobby," nodded Jacob.

"Well, Jake, I don't know yet if I'm glad to meet you. But it's done, so we'll have to make the best of it, I reckon. You stay here and I'll git the rest of us."

As the little tribe assembled, Jacob learned they lined up by age. Bobby introduced each one by first name only, and by age.

"This here's Doyle, 15 years," announced Bobby. Doyle was a half head taller than Bobby, and quite thin, observed Jacob.

"So how old are you?" asked Jacob.

"Sixteen," replied Bobby. "I'm the oldest."

"This here's Emmie, fourteen," continued Bobby.

"Well, I'm past fourteen and a half," replied Emmie.

"Okay, y'all. Just let me get through this, will ya'?" Bobby was impatient. They shouldn't be hanging out in the outer room with searchers out, but they hadn't voted on the newcomer yet, so they couldn't take him back into the living quarters yet.

"Now this is James, fourteen, and Lily and Violet are twins, both thirteen, and Reggie is the youngest. He's ten—and a half!"

"I am very glad to meet you all," said Jacob, "and I want to thank you for allowing me into your group. My name is Jacob."

"Well, there's a thing," said Bobby. "You ain't in our group yet. We have to vote on you. Our folks laid down some rules before we left home. They said we had to stick to them, or we would fail. One rule was we needed to discuss important matters and take a vote. Like who would lead. No one person was to bully or dominate the others just because he was older or bigger."

"Sounds wise," replied Jacob. "What are some of your other rules?"

"Not many," said Bobby. "We are supposed to love God more than anything else and obey the Good Book. And we are supposed to treat others the way we want to be treated. We aren't to breed relation or same sex, and only breed if we stand before God and make a promise to each other and to God, and not breed anybody else but the one we make a promise to. We had to memorize the Ten Commandments and obey them. No lyin' or murderin' or stealin'—like that— s'bout it."

Jacob nodded his head. "Good rules. So do you have a Bible?"

"Yep. They sent us with one. We still have it. Thing is, ain't nobody left who can really understand it. We've been in the timber almost three years. All the older kids who could read good are dead. And me an' Doyle never was any good at reading even when we was in school. The youngers kinda lost it with no practice," said Bobby. "We just been trying to keep alive."

"What happened to the older kids?" asked Jacob. "How many of you came here altogether?"

"Eleven. They died from different things. We all got sick 'bout the first year we were here. Johnny and Mary died. The rest of us finally got better, though. Then Jed went out huntin' and never came back. And Colin got bit by a rattler and died."

"Why didn't your parents come with you?" asked Jacob.

" Well, they figgered we would have a better chance on our own. There were babies and old folk, you see. We wouldn't take the vaccine 'causen of the stuff they put in it—using parts of aborted babies, an' changin' the genes, which means changin' us as human bein's, and the sterilization drugs and then the trackin' mark of the Beast. Our folks said wern't no takin' that, 'cause we'd lose our souls. Said everybody's gonna die sometime, but losing your soul in hell is forever. No, sir. Better to trade your life for heaven than to live a little longer on this here earth and spend eternity in hell forever. That's what they taught us. Choose God's side," Bobby finished.

"So you have been here surviving off the woods all this time?" asked Jacob.

"Purdy much," replied Bobby. "We went back to the village after the first year. Nobody was there. Just the graves of the babies. They had decided to not let the troops take the little ones, since they would use them for body parts while they were still alive. So they put them to sleep and gave them a good, Christian burial. When the troops came, they just killed the old folks 'cause they wouldn't take the mark and wouldn't be able to work in the camps. They didn't get buried. They just left them where they shot them. We took their bones to the timber behind the village and buried them. Our folks said they couldn't escape with the little ones, and we couldn't probably keep the young ones alive. Most of us was raised in the forest, but our pa's took us into the forest and trained us and got us set up. Then one day when we heard the trucks comin', they yelled for us to run! Not all of us got away who was supposed to, and one got away who was supposed to stay—Reggie. He is a good, fast runner, and when we got here, he was right behind us. He's a good little hunter, too!" Reggie grinned great big at the praise, but Jacob noticed tears had run down his face while Bobby told the story, and as he looked around, saw tears in all of their eyes.

"So what's your story?" asked Bobby.

"They killed my mom," replied Jacob. "My grandfather is a genetic biologist, and refused to work for the government doing the kind of research you described. So after they threatened him and kept him from working anywhere else, and took all our money, they finally killed my mom to try to force him, so he and my dad and I went into hiding. When word came that they were coming to our camp, they got us out first to keep my grandfather safe from torture and drugs to make him do what they wanted. Some people got us and were going to bring us to this camp, but they were caught and detained. They had told us to come on to bring the supplies back to the Farm if they got caught, so we did, and have been here for a several months." Jacob realized he had just summed up his nightmarish existence of the last few years in a few brief sentences. Unreal. "So what about the vote?" he asked.

One by one the citizens voted. Stones were placed in yes or no bowls out of sight, then counted by Reggie and Lily and Doyle. They came back and Reggie announced that all of the stones were in the yes bowl!

Chapter ELEVEN

A s they showed Jacob into the living quarters, they heard a huge explosion and the earth under them shook, and the cave over them sifted dirt down on them.

All the children stood stone still. Should they run? Was the cave going to collapse? What was that booming? They had never heard thunder deep in the living quarters before, and certainly no thunder that caused falling dirt from the ceiling.

"Has this ever happened before?" asked Jacob.

"No, never," replied Bobby.

"I don't think it was natural," said Jacob. "I think it was artillery or bombs, or something."

They agreed to stay put in the cave for a couple of days and let whatever was going on outside settle. They had enough if they rationed their food, and they had a spring in the cave for water. That was one of the main reasons their parents had selected this particular cave in the forest—that, and the very narrow, hidden entrance. The explosions troubled Jacob—a lot. He couldn't tell anything from underground which direction they came from, how far away they were, or anything. He really wanted to go out, but the forest could be crawling with troops. He couldn't risk getting caught out again and putting the camp or this little band of cave dwellers at risk any more than he already had.

They were all settling down to small chores and handcrafts. They apparently had done this drill before. Then he spied the Good Book, as they had called it. He asked permission to look at it. As he sat reading it, some gathered around him, watching. Jacob looked up.

"Yes?" asked Jacob.

They all stood silently, shuffling their feet a bit. Finally, Lily asked, "Would you read it to us, Jacob?"

Surprised at his thoughtlessness, Jacob said, "Of course. I should have offered. Where would you like me to read?"

Reggie answered, "Jesus!" at the same time Emmie said, "Start at the beginning!"

Jacob thought for a moment and then said, "How about this—we start at the beginning in Genesis and read how God created the universe and then we can turn back to the New Testament and read about Jesus for awhile, and finish with a Psalm and a Proverb?"

They looked at each other like, "That was clear as mud," and shrugged their shoulders.

"Let's try it and see what you think," said Jacob. "We can always change it."

As they read, Bobby turned his attention to Jacob. Jacob noticed, and asked Bobbly if he had a question.

" I remember my dad saying we had to have faith in God," replied Bobby. "But I never knew what he meant. I just heard the folks in church talkin' about it, and never paid it much mind. I don't know what it is, so how do I know if I have it? We used to go to church. We learnt the Ten Commandments and our parents sent us with the other rules to live by. Love God more than anything else and treat other people the way we want to be treated. Is that faith?"

" That's a good start toward faith," said Jacob. "My dad is a Bible teacher and he said the Bible tells us faith begins with believing God. We just read about how God created everything and about Adam and Eve. Did they believe God?" asked Jacob.

"No!" replied Violet. "They believed the serpent and disobeyed God."

"Right, Violet. They believed in God, because He made them and came and visited with them in the garden. But when the serpent said God had lied to them and that God was keeping something good from them, he implied God was trying to keep them down and didn't really love them. And they listened to the serpent, who is really a fallen angel who had turned against God and wanted to take God's place. He hates the children God made. God made them to be like Himself—God's children—and the serpent tricked them into listening to him instead of obeying God. He knew that when they disobeyed God, they would die spiritually, just like God had said. It separated them from God that very day. And eventually their bodies would die also. That fallen angel's name was Satan and he tricked Adam and Even into the death of their spirit by their disobedience and the death of their bodies, and to be punished in hell forever with Satan for their disobedience."

"So why should we have faith in God," asked Doyle "if we're doomed to hell?"

"Well, God really loved His children and had a plan. God had to do what was right, because He is righteous and just, and sin must be punished. But He is also full of mercy and love and forgiveness. The plan was that God, as Jesus, would come and live a perfect life on earth with His people without sinning. Then He could die in the place of everyone who believed in Him, so those children who love Him could live with Him forever." Jacob felt his explanation was incomplete.

"So Jesus died for everybody's sins? How does that work? One for everybody?" asked Doyle.

"Yes," said Jacob. "It works because God said justice is satisfied with the death of one perfect man, because sin entered the world because of the sin of one man, Adam. Everybody sins because they inherited the sin nature from Adam. So Jesus can take away the sin of the world with His one, perfect sacrifice."

"So everybody is saved?" asked Lily, with her brow furrowed. "Even those bad people who killed our mommies and daddies and sisters and brothers?"

"This is where faith comes in," said Jacob. "God said everyone who believes God can be saved. It's like everyone has the same chance that Adam and Eve had in the beginning. Each one of us can tell God that we are sorry for our sin and we want to love and obey Him and live with Him forever because we believe Jesus died for our sin so we can be cleaned—or made righteous again—by His death in our place."

"But we still die," said Doyle.

"Our bodies do," agreed Jacob. "But God has promised that our bodies will be resurrected and we will have a new spiritual body that will never die. Jesus said if we believe, we will live, even if we die."

"Tell that to the old folks' bones we buried!" shot back Dolye.

"So we're back to faith," said Jacob. "God said we have to believe Him and not be like Adam and Eve."

"Maybe they were right. Why should we believe Him? Where is this good God? All I see is evil everywhere," challenged Doyle.

"And that is the crux of it," said Jacob. "But God said there is a basis for our faith. It is not some blind leap off a cliff."

"Hmph," said Doyle. "What basis is that? All I see are old stories that don't prove anything."

"First of all, God says He made everything—out of nothing. That He spoke it and it came into being out of nothing. We just read it in Genesis," said Jacob.

"So? No way to prove it. Besides, what does that have to do with faith?" challenged Doyle.

"Well," replied Jacob, "it had to come from somewhere, and anywhere you start, you have to start with something, and where did that something come from? It all has order—outer space, the atom and molecules, the cell, the eye—they didn't all just happen. God is the only answer that makes sense. So if God has the power to speak the universe into being, He also has the power to raise people from the dead if He made them in the first place."

Doyle just stared at Jacob; then nodded. "Go on."

"Well," said Jacob, the Bible says God is good and He cannot lie. Lying is a sin and God calls out sin; He doesn't sin. So if He makes a promise, He will keep it. What God says, He means, and He can and will do it. And He promised His children eternal life. And He made an oath on top of the promise—that's like a contract, it's law. Then He gave the evidence in real life. He raised Jesus from the dead to never die again. Jesus went up to heaven before their eyes. And He said He's coming back again and will raise the dead and any of His children who are still alive when He comes back to make all things right again, they will be instantly changed into their perfect body and go to meet Jesus in the air."

"And you believe that?" asked Doyle.

"Yes, I do," responded Jacob. "I never realized how much until right now."

"So you are saying every person has to decide if they believe what you just said, yes or no, and that will decide if you have faith to be saved. To believe God, or not to believe God and be a rebel in hell, that is the question. And you show if you believe God by obeying Him."

"That's pretty much it," said Jacob. "But that obeying is a process. Our heart is changed when we believe, but being saved is a process to continue to be transformed to be like Jesus our whole lives. We must participate in that process all along the way, ask forgiveness when we mess up and continue on. Jesus said 'He who remains faithful to the end will be saved.'"

Jacob saw Bobby in the recesses of the shadows, sitting quietly, watching this exchange between Jacob and Doyle. Bobby looked at Jacob and simply nodded his head. Jacob decided to leave it at that with the two older boys to give them time to think about it. He turned to the younger kids, who were sitting on blankets on the cave floor.

"Any questions?" he asked.

"Do you just tell God you believe?" asked Emmie.

"That's right," responded Jacob. "God is a person, and we are made in His image. He is not human with a body like ours, He is spirit. He is everywhere and He is all-powerful. He knows everything. He says He hears us when we talk to Him and we can know Him and He knows us. He promised if we are His children, He will come and live in us so He can be with us always and we'll never be alone. He said His Holy Spirit will live in us and teach us and comfort us, and convict our conscience when we do wrong so we can confess it to God and ask forgiveness. And another one of His promises is that if we do that truly in our hearts, He will forgive us and clean us up in our spirits. And He promises if we need direction and wisdom, all we have to do is ask and He will give it gladly. God wants us to seek to know Him, and He will open His heart to us and let us find Him—to really know Him."

"What do I say?" asked Emmie.

"Yes—what do I say?" chimed in the other five.

"So are each of you wanting to tell God you have faith in Him and want to be saved from sin and rebellion to eternal life as His children in heaven forever?" asked Jacob.

All five enthusiastically prayed with Jacob. He laid his hands on each one and prayed for them to receive the Holy Spirit. As he looked up, he saw Bobby kneeling by a rock in the shadows, praying. Jacob walked over to him and asked Bobby, "You, too?"

"Yes," said Bobby. "I believe God."

After they prayed together, Jacob laid his hands on Bobby to receive the Holy Spirit.

Doyle had left the room.

Chapter TWELVE

Ivy, Evan and Tony were inducted into the work camp. They had male and female sleeping quarters, so Ivy was separated from her dad and Tony. She never felt so alone or so scared. They made her change into a prisoner uniform. It wasn't a drab black and gray striped uniform like she had seen pictures of the World War II death camps in Germany. Although they came and took all of those history books out of the school library. Then they did away with the libraries all together. Ivy hated that. She loved the library filled with row upon row of books. As her world became smaller and smaller with all the pandemics (Dad called them plagues) and the restrictions they brought with them, the books let her get away to other places and other times. Then they were gone. All their school work was done on computer and books, reading material, all research and reference materials were accessed online. The government controlled all the information. Books were to be turned in, like the cash had been earlier. Supposedly, that was to keep students from using "outdated" materials that were no longer valid. Or didn't say what the government dictated, is what Dad said. That world seemed a lifetime away. Here she was in a bright orange jump suit that could be seen a mile away. Even if she could figure out a way to escape, she'd be caught immediately. *These things probably glow in the dark.* She didn't realize she need not to complain about that, because very soon it would be covered in dirt and grime, and look like gray rags.

A guard showed up at the door of the bunk room to escort Ivy to an interrogation room. They mostly wanted general information this time and then took her to her work detail. She kept looking for any sign of her dad and Tony, but didn't see them anywhere the first day. *God, please keep them safe. Please take care of them. Help us all be faithful to the end, whenever that end may be. I look to Your coming, Jesus. Come Lord Jesus. I never really understood the cry of that verse. Yes, Lord Jesus, Come! How many people over the millennia have cried that prayer as they waited beneath the coliseum to be eaten by lions, waited in line for the guillotine, were locked inside a church burning down around them, or waited their turn to be hung on a cross, or burned at the stake, or carted off into slavery like I have been today. Jesus, help me to be worthy of the honor to suffer for Your name's sake and the memory of my mother!*

Evan and Tony were told to change and were then immediately separated. Tony felt very still inside. Waiting. It surprised him. Something inside his head said he should be freaking out. But he wasn't. He wondered what was next, but had no anxiety, just a quiet stillness, waiting. Then he realized he was waiting for God, and a presence filled both the room and Tony's heart with a deep and wonderful peace and he was filled with joy. Since his talk with God by the edge of the pond after his parents had been taken, Tony had drawn close to God and learned to know His presence and to hear His voice. He studied God's word and learned the Holy Spirit would speak to Tony through it, but also would bring God's word to mind at various times—like He would check Tony if he would have a selfish thought or bad attitude. He learned to depend on the voice of God inside of him when he didn't know what to do. But this—this peace transported Tony to another world. He felt like Jesus was enveloping him in his arms and comforting him. Tony remembered His words by the pond, "*I will never leave you or forsake you. I will be with you always, even to the end of the age. I will live in you. I love you and died so you can be with me forever, Tony. I call you by name.*" And then Tony heard His voice, "*You are mine, and I am yours.*" Whether it was audible, or not, Tony didn't know—he just knew it was real.

Evan wasn't worried about himself, but he was concerned about Ivy and Tony. He felt both responsible for their welfare and at the same time helpless to do anything about it. "God!" he cried out in the conflict of his mind.

"I am here, Evan. And I am with Tony and Ivy, also. Just stand and wait upon me. You shall be my witnesses. I will give you what you are to say. I will bring to completion the good work I have begun in you. Be faithful to the end. Remember, 'Do not fear those who kill the body but are unable to kill the soul; but rather fear Him who is able to destroy both soul and body in hell.'"

"Father, I am yours to do with as you will. Help me be faithful. Make Ivy and Tony wise and strong and filled with your Spirit to overcome. Give them courage and joy and see you high and lifted up—the King of Kings and Lord of Lords!"

"Yes, Evan, they will see Me. They will see their reward."

Evan felt like he heard God smile when He spoke. Like there was more meaning behind those simple words.

Evan suffered through all the interrogations, and yet he lived. Even the serums they gave him produced no results. He clearly did not know where any of the other Farms were. In some ways he thought it would be better to die and go to Jesus. What a relief that would be! But he did not want to leave Ivy and Tony alone. So he thanked God for the ragged, fragile life that remained in him. He thought of Louisa. His heart ached to think of her crash and all of her suffering just to face these devils who tortured her to death. God, don't let my heart go there. Help me! I can't let Satan steal my peace with unforgiveness. I pray for my enemies—sometimes I forget they are under the delusion of our enemy. They don't know what they are doing. They are like zombies following his orders. If there is a way to free them, I pray you will deliver them. They shoved Evan through the door of his cell and he fell onto the bare concrete floor and passed out.

Ivy looked for her father in the feeding room. Then she found Tony. They knew better than to try to fight for some gruel, so they slumped down and leaned against the wall.

"Where's Dad?" asked Ivy, concern in her voice.

"They came and took him this morning before we left the room. I haven't seen him since," replied Tony.

"God, please keep him safe and give him strength. I am so worried about him! Father, he keeps getting thinner and thinner, and seems so weak at times," Ivy prayed in response to Tony's answer. "We have lost everybody—please, we don't want to lose Daddy, too! Have mercy on him and us, Lord. Help us be lights and faithful followers of Jesus no matter what happens. Amen."

They both just sat and stared at the floor for a few minutes without saying anything. Then Tony, quietly nodding his head, as though hearing a conversation no one else heard, said, "Okay, we have work to do if we are to be lights. And it will keep our minds occupied. God doesn't want us to waste energy worrying about something we can't do anything about. And He knows we don't have any energy to waste—let's make it count!" With that, Tony began singing and Ivy joined him. Some of the other slaves drew closer. Others, exhausted and hungry, just stayed put but joined in from where they sat on the floor. Others, sullen, just glared and cursed under their breath. The gentle voices reverberated off the concrete walls and floor in a mystical choir lifting praise to God, almost bell-like with human words. Some songs spoke of the return of Jesus Messiah. Some were simple praise and trust and adoration. After the brutes ate their fill, the rest were able to take in some nourishment before returning to work. When they returned from work many hours later, Ivy and Tony shared Bible stories with the other slaves while the brutes filled their bellies first. The door opened, and Evan shuffled through it. He looked like death walking. When Ivy saw him, she let out a little cry. It was a cry of relief mixed with alarm at his physical condition. Evan looked up at her cry and gratitude swept over his face to see his daughter. She ran to his open arms and stood still just in front of him to allow him to embrace her in a way that would cause the least pain.

"I heard your songs this noon through the ventilation system. They helped me, daughter, and I think it influenced the agents, as well, although I doubt they realized it. They soon ended their business after the singing began. Thank you. It gave me strength to endure."

"Oh, Daddy, I prayed God would give you strength. I didn't know you could hear us," replied Ivy.

Evan had noticed lately that Ivy had returned to using "Daddy" when addressing him. It had been years since "Dad" had replaced "Daddy." But now he was "Daddy," again. In some ways since their detainment, she had become much stronger and bolder, but in others, more childlike and tender and perceptive.

She watched others around her to see how she could help them with a kind word or a gentle touch, a bit of conversation, cleaning a wound, or a scrap of bread saved in her sleeve from a meal. Evan watched Christ grow in this slight child of mercy, and it blessed him. He remembered her selfish impetuousness, bickering with Tony. How they had both grown in the Lord. Their bodies were wasting, as was his, but God had used these circumstances to refine them in ways that peace and prosperity never could have. These two children were truly gems being polished by the Master's hand. Evan gazed into his daughter's eyes looking up into his own, and he worshipped God.

"The Lord answers our prayers in ways we would never imagine," replied Evan finally.

They walked over to Tony who was watching them from their "spot" away from the feeding table where they could have their backs to the wall while they waited for the brutes to finish eating.

"Kids—I guess I shouldn't call you that—you are more mature than most adults—I need you to know that I believe I may not be here much longer."

He lifted his hand to quiet their protests. "Just listen, okay? If there is one thing we have learned, it is that these bodies are not going to last forever. I'm not old for a man, but my body is wearing out. I have prayed and asked God to let me stay to be with you, and He has until now, but I have a sense that my time to depart is near. Something that is on my heart is that there are people in here—especially the guards—who need to hear that God loves them and there is forgiveness and salvation in Jesus. We have spoken to many of the prisoners, and many have come to Christ. Many of those have already departed. I am so grateful for God's mercy. But we are to love our enemies, too. Even those who persecute us. Jesus said to pray for them, and we have. But if we have the truth and do not tell them the truth, and they die in their sin, then God says their blood is on our hands and He will judge us for it. So I must speak, even though I will probably die for it. I don't want you to grieve with broken hearts. I want you to grieve with gratitude that God has made me faithful to the end. And in faith and hope that will never disappoint, because God, who cannot lie, has made us a promise of eternal life with Him. The God who made the universe by speaking it into being and resurrecting the dead, is able to deliver on His promise. We have a sure hope. The time is coming. We do not see it now, but we believe God. Jesus is near. I believe you may very well be alive and remain at His coming to be caught up with the resurrected dead to meet the Lord in the air. You may very well see Him coming on the clouds with the blast of the trumpet of God and a great shout of the archangel. Kids—hold on tight to Him, no matter what threats and dangers you face. Jim Elliot was right when he said, 'He is no fool who gives up what he cannot keep to gain what he cannot lose.' Remember that. That is overcoming evil. That is the victory."

Most had cleared away from the feeding table so they rose and gathered food for some who had no strength to feed themselves. They sat with them and prayed for them, knowing that some would not make it through the cold night on the concrete floor in the cells. Tony, Ivy, and Evan ate what scraps were left after everyone was fed and gave thanks to God their provider.

Chapter THIRTEEN

Two days passed. No intruders, no helicopters, no more explosions. They decided two of them would venture out to see what had happened and try to find some food. Jacob and Doyle were selected in case they ran into trouble. Bobby objected, but he knew in his heart he needed to stay as leader of the little flock in case the others didn't come back. Jacob and Doyle were both capable in the timber and getting food.

They set out with a little dried bread and dried meat, and each had a flask of water. Nothing seemed out of the ordinary that would explain the sounds of explosions they had heard, but they did come across large truck tracks by the service road, and many boot tracks that spread out across the forest. This place had been crawling with troops—looking for Jacob, no doubt. A prayer of thanksgiving and praise flew from his heart and his mind to the One who had hid his soul in the cleft of the rock at the moment he had prayed.

"It's a good thing you found our cave!" whispered Doyle. "They were everywhere!"

"I prayed just before I found it," said Jacob. "I know God protected me."

"Why doesn't He protect everyone?" asked Doyle.

"I don't know why God does everything He does," replied Jacob. "I just know He's a lot smarter than me and He has a plan and it will be completed. I trust Him."

"How can He be good if this is His plan? Satan is ruling the world. How can that be God's plan?"

"God is a righteous judge. He is letting Satan by his own evil actions condemn himself before the great cloud of witnesses in heaven. God is letting each person prove their faithfulness through the trials we go through, producing the evidence that will either acquit or condemn us. Life is a test, Doyle. A test to determine who is on the Lord's side and who is not. When I come up against hard things, I remind myself—this is a test—and ask God to help me faithfully pass the test."

"That sucks," snapped Doyle.

"I used to think that, too," replied Jacob. "My grandpa reminded me that in the whole scheme of things, our suffering here is light and temporary compared to eternity in hell. And the joy of the promise of heaven is so great that it can't even compare to anything we go through here. In other words, it's worth it. I have counted the cost and it is worth it—nothing compares to the promise I have in God."

"You really believe this stuff, don't you?"

"Yep. I just don't understand why you wouldn't," replied Jacob.

"I do," said Doyle.

"What!" replied Jacob, and he quickly lowered his voice.

"What you said makes sense," said Doyle. "I have heard a lot of this since I was little. My dad was the preacher, but I don't remember him giving the 'why' of faith, or maybe I just wasn't listening. But I did have questions. God just seemed very ineffective when I saw what was happening in the world, or He wasn't good, or wasn't all those omni things we were told He is. There just seemed to be a big disconnect between doctrine and life."

"Well, it's our time to reconnect doctrine and life, Doyle. It's our time to live our life out in faith in the living God, however long that is. It's time to be the real thing!"

Jacob and Doyle arrived at the Farm with no encounters with humans. Jacob stood at the edge of the compound in stunned disbelief. The compound had been leveled. Well, the mystery of the explosions had been cleared up. The devastation was complete. There were no bodies left on the grounds, except the dog. They must have taken them for identification purposes. They would want to know if they had killed Grandfather. Jacob walked over to Leroy. He rolled his body with his foot. Bullet wounds. He wasn't killed in the blast. How had he survived the bombs? And why did they bother to shoot the dog afterward? Unless Leroy attacked. But Leroy only attacked—if you could call tackling people and then standing over them wagging his tail an attack—if he was defending Tony. Jacob stood and made a slow circle, examining the camp with expectant eyes. There—the open door of the root cellar. Jacob cautiously walked toward it, examining footprints in the dust. Trooper boots, a man's dress shoes, like Evan wore. He had said in their rush to leave home, he forgot to bring another pair of shoes. Ivy's flip flops. Tennis shoes. Those would be Tony's. He stayed home from hunting to help Evan with a project building shelves for the kitchen so they could store more supplies in the house and not have to make so many trips back and forth to the root cellar. They all must have been in the root cellar when the bombs fell and it saved them. They were found afterward by the troops and the dog went into defense mode. Took a few rounds, by the look of it. But they all walked away from the root cellar. Jacob followed the foot prints through the dust of the devastation toward the road. Truck tracks. The prints stopped there. They must have taken them into custody. *God have mercy!*

Jacob had been totally lost in his thoughts since they entered the camp. He looked up to see Doyle watching him from a fallen log. He walked over to Doyle.

"I was just remembering the first time we walked back into our village," said Doyle. "Are you okay?"

"I will be. This had to be an air strike. I don't think anyone suffered. Except maybe the three who were in the root cellar. I think Grandfather and my dad were probably killed instantly with the rest. The ones who were captured are who I'm worried about now."

"You're not supposed to worry."

"You know what I mean. The rest are in heaven. But Ivy and Tony and Evan may still be suffering. So I will pray for them," replied Jacob.

"How do you know some were saved and who they are?" asked Doyle.

Jacob explained the story of the day he went out hunting in the woods and had to go farther than usual, and that his friend Tony was unable to go because he was helping Evan. They walked and Jacob showed the footprints to Doyle. As they stood at the top of the cellar steps, they both looked at each other and started down. The stash they found would be a huge boon to the cave dwellers. *Thank you, Lord!*

Chapter FOURTEEN

Evan, Ivy, and Tony spent the last night they expected to be together in prayer and worship. Evan's plan was to preach the salvation message right after lunch tomorrow, providing he lived that long. His health had deteriorated quickly the past couple of weeks. It was time. He sat with his arm around Ivy until the curfew sounded. They shared memories and stories of better times, the blessings that God had provided in the work camp by saving many people, and the privilege of ministering to so many suffering people. They even shared laughs over some Leroy stories—their hero dog. Evan hugged Tony and reflected on how much he had changed since they came to the Farm. He had become a young man of character with a heart after God. Maybe his body was a little scrawny and frail, but he was a spiritual strong man.

And Ivy—his dear Ivy—looking so much like her mother... he felt the tears well up. He grabbed her tightly in his arms and kissed her hair as a few tears escaped from his eyes. His chest felt so tight, he could barely breathe. The guard came to the door and barked a command at them. All three called down God's blessing on him and headed to their sleeping quarters.

The next day, Evan prayed all morning for the strength to make it back to the feeding room for the noon meal. It was especially raucous that day, so Evan didn't even try to preach over the din. He noticed a newcomer and would liked to have visited with him, but he rested to gather his strength before they were lined up to go back to work. Silently he prayed for God's anointing, and began, "Jesus said, 'I AM the Way, the Truth, and the Life, no one comes to the Father except through Me...'"

At the end of the work day, the newcomer came and sat down beside Ivy and Tony while they waited for the brutes to eat first. They cautiously introduced themselves as Lee and Roy, but then began to open up after the kind words that the stranger spoke about Evan's death that noon.

All of a sudden, one of the other workers began yelling at his wife and beating her. When his two sons began fighting and the younger one screamed, the father flew into more of a rage, and yelling, "Shut up!" he slammed the boy's head against the concrete wall. The boy slumped dead to the floor right next to Ivy. She cried out and reached for the boy, but immediately realized his skull was crushed when his blood filled her lap. Soon a guard dragged the boy out by his leg, while his mother sat in zombie-like silence, staring at the wall. Ivy crumpled in a heap, sobbing for her young friend, for her father, for her mother, for all the injustice and evil assaulting her from every side.

The stranger moved from the wall and positioned himself between Ivy and Tony and the menacing shadows across the room. He reached out his hand and laid it on Ivy's head with the words, "Peace, daughter. My peace I give to you. Do not let your heart be troubled. Believe in God, believe also in Me. In my Father's house are many dwelling places; if it were not so I would have told you; for I go to prepare a place for you. If I go to prepare a place for you, I will come again and receive you to Myself, that where I am, there you may be also."

"Jesus said to her, 'I am the resurrection and the life; he who believes in Me will live even if he dies, and everyone who lives and believes in Me will never die. Do you believe this?'"

Ivy looked down at her young friend's blood in her lap—the young boy she had just led to the Lord two days ago. "Yes, Lord," she replied as she looked up into the eyes of the kind stranger in front of her. "I know you. I know your voice."

"Yes, Ivy, we know each other," replied the stranger.

He turned to Tony. "Be ready. I am coming soon. Be ready!"